Vagrant

Gabe Thompson

Vagrant

By Gabe Thompson
© 2016 Vagrant
Swartz Creek, MI 48473
Cover design by Clarissa Yeo

Tell-Tale Publishing   Stargazer Imprint

Printed by

Tell-Tale Publishing Group, LLC
5714 Peri St.
Swartz Creek, MI 48473

STARGAZER

www.tell-talepublishing.com

VAGRANT

Chapter One

"I smell gas." Logan Hall glanced over his shoulder at his young partner, Raj Kumaran. "Gas can blow into these tunnels and turn you into a crispy critter."

They were on their knees crawling through a dark, narrow tunnel cut through the living rock deep under the super city of New York. "We better look for an exit."

"I don't smell anything," Raj said.

"You'll learn. It smells like broccoli."

"What's broccoli?"

"You never ate broccoli? It's a vegetable. The Professor grows it."

"Nope. I hate all veggies."

Logan laughed. "Well start eating them or you'll be a shrimp for the rest of your life." This was Raj's first trip. The kid was only ten. Logan was a much more mature and experienced seventeen. He spotted a side tunnel ahead and scuttled to it as the smell of gas grew more intense. Tunnel gas, traps, Sniffer Hounds, cave-ins, Ears, these were all dangers every tunnel rat faced when they went on a mission.

"Here," he shot over his shoulder as he dived into a crevasse that led to a much larger tunnel.

The larger tunnel ran parallel to the Loop, a huge high-speed rail system running through enormous Plexiglas tubes like a Habitrail. The system ran from New York north to Boston and even beyond to Montreal, Canada, annexed six years ago by the U.S. It ran south all the way to Richmond, Virginia. New York had become one gigantic city reaching west into Pennsylvania where he'd heard one day it would connect to the Loop in another super city, New Chicago.

1

They ran hunched over through intense dark. The tiny light in Logan's helmet, a retrofitted bicycle helmet, illuminated the uneven rock of the tunnel floor and rough-hewn sides. Logan could see without it, probably a mutation or maybe his eyes had adapted to a lower level of light because, while he'd been born above ground, he'd been underground since his father brought him there when he was seven to save them from deportation. But Raj was still just a kid, and this was his first mission, so Logan had it set on high.

When they reached a junction, Logan stopped and held his hand out behind his body to halt Raj. He held one finger to his lips. Over his head, a tiny green light blinked. It was an Ear. He pointed to it so Raj would notice. The government was always listening even down here.

When the eerie scream of the high-speed train approaching filled the tunnel, Logan took the north passage running under Central Park West toward Washington Heights. They ran lightly through the much larger tunnel until Logan heard the sound he most feared. He froze and Raj ran into him. Logan heard a scrabbling sound in the tunnel ahead and recognized it as a Sniffer Hound, robots programmed to locate, capture or even kill anything alive in the tunnels.

He grabbed Raj's arm and dragged him to a ladder running up and into a narrow tube. He shoved Raj ahead of him. "Climb," he ordered.

Raj scrambled up the rusty rungs of the ladder like a monkey with Logan following on his heels. Below, the scrabbling sounds had increased along with a high-pitched whistle. The Sniffer was calling more robotic killers to the hunt. They'd been scented.

The tube led to a manhole. Logan pointed and whispered, "Push."

Raj pushed and the metal disc slid open, rotating counterclockwise. Below them, Logan sensed the Sniffer using its suction cups to climb up the tube. Each cup made a distinct sound as it released and attached to a new spot. It wasn't loud, but Logan dreamed about that sound and would never mistake it. They scrambled out and Logan gave the manhole cover a shove. It rotated back into place and snapped shut with a metallic clank.

They emerged into a narrow crawl space, the ceiling only inches above their heads. Logan rolled to his left until he felt the edge, swung one leg over, and dropped onto a catwalk. Raj followed, his eyes round and terrified. "Where are we?"

"Sewer," Logan said. The catwalk was ancient, rusted through in many places and rickety. It clattered as Logan inched along. Below them a river of thick sludge ran through a wide canal. The fetid stench rose in a miasma of steam. The tunnel was so old it was constructed of faded red bricks coated with a thick layer of green slime. "Don't touch the green stuff," Logan whispered.

They inched down the catwalk to a ledge. Logan stepped onto the ledge and pressed his back against the bricks. He sidestepped to another metal ladder, grabbed the third rung and swung onto it. Raj followed. The ladder went up to the roof and stopped. Logan shoved his shoulders into a tunnel that opened in the roof. It was barely wide enough for them to squeeze through. The tube was stained black and smelled of blood and death. Logan planted both his feet on one side of the tube and pushed his shoulders into the wall. When he felt secure he began to inch up the tube. Raj had more trouble and was slow to follow. He finally figured out the chimney climb and caught up to Logan. When they reached the top, Logan pushed on a metal grate. It lifted and Logan stuck his head through into the dank chill of a cooler. He struggled to get his shoulders out and then fell onto his butt breathing heavily. "That was close. I hate that tube."

Raj lifted his eyebrows. "What was it?"

"It's a drain for the morgue. All kinds of gross crap goes down there."

Raj rolled onto his knees and peered down the drain. "You're kidding?"

"Nope."

"What were you so scared of back there?"

"A Sniffer Hound. The Sniffer was almost on us. They trap you and use an electrified net to catch you or if they fail to catch you they use flame throwers to incinerate your body into a small pile of ashes."

"Wow! I didn't hear anything."

"You'll learn." Logan clambered to his feet, slinging the empty pack over his shoulder.

"Where the heck are we?"

Logan clicked on the helmet light.

"That's disgusting!" Raj's eyes were wide with horror. "Are they dead?"

They were in the cooler of the basement morgue in Mt. Sinai General Hospital. Bodies on gurneys, covered in white sheets, surrounded them.

Logan smacked Raj on the top of the head with the flat of his hand. "Of course, I told you, this is a freaking morgue."

He shoved the closest gurney at Raj and laughed when Raj squeaked. "They can't hurt you, dude, they're dead."

Logan opened the heavy door to the cold locker slowly and peered out. It was night. He knew only a skeleton crew manned the morgue at night because there was a shortage of qualified help in the cities. There was a shortage of trained workers all over the world. Ever since John Demaris discovered what he named the warp drive after the hyper drive in Star Trek, and space travel to far worlds became a reality, the government had been rounding up every able-bodied man on the planet and shipping them off-world to work the mines of faraway galaxies. That's where Logan's father was. He'd been caught and shipped off to what the Mole People called Planet 666, Gliese 667, a brown planet with enough water to maintain life and lots and lots of gold.

"Come on," he said to Raj. "We have to make the pickup in five minutes."

They found hospital scrubs in a cupboard and put them on. Dressed like every hospital employee, the two boys slipped through the dark hallways of the hospital, took the stairs to the ground floor and then ducked outside. Logan led the way around the building to the alley in the back and the row of garbage containers behind the Emergency Room. He shoved Raj behind one marked with a red biohazard tag and squatted down to wait.

"What're we waiting for now?" Raj asked.

Logan took out half of a cigarette and lit it with a match he took from a plastic bag. He inhaled deeply and Raj shook his head. "Why do you do that?"

"Cause my dad did. He loved a good smoke and so does I. It's relaxing to me. I get pretty cranked runnin' through the tunnels and you need a calm head about you to survive."

The glass doors of the ER slid open with a sucking sound and Logan peaked around the edge of the trash container and there she was . . . his angel.

"Wow!" Raj breathed. "What a dynamite chick."

"Don't even look at her, mole. She's so far above us, she don't even exist. She's a vision, an angel from above."

"Well, your angel is toting a white plastic bag. Is that our package?"

Logan nodded. When Raj leaned across Logan to get a better look, he accidentally shoved Logan who reached out to catch himself from falling on his face and banged the edge of the container. The angel gasped and looked right into his eyes.

She was so beautiful. Her long black hair swung over one shoulder when she bent over to look at him through the clearest brown eyes Logan had ever seen. They were filled with the innocence of the protected, a girl who had never eaten roasted rat or run for her life into tunnels so deep beneath the city you encountered an even worse nightmare, the Worms. And then it hit him. Her pupils were small, her gaze focused. Unlike the majority of the people who lived topside, she looked straight.

"Who are you?" his angel asked.

Logan stood up and brushed the top layer of filth off his borrowed scrubs. He straightened his back and shoved a lock of dirty blond hair out of his eyes. "I'm Logan. I come from down there." He pointed to his feet then grabbed Raj by the shoulder. "This is my little buddy, Raj."

She backed up rapidly still clutching the white-plastic bag. "You're one of *them*? You live underground?"

Logan thrust his well-developed chest out and lifted his chin. "Yeah, we're not animals you know. We're people, too."

Shayna Nagata was in shock. All her life she'd been bombarded with horror stories about the people who lived underground. The homeless, the poor, the mutated animals no one wanted would come out of the manholes at night and feed on the children of the rich and privileged. Her parents had drummed it into her head. Never, ever, ever talk to anyone you think does not belong above ground. They have no chips. They have no credit and no job. They kill people like her and steal children away to feed on under the earth.

She reached out a shaking hand and touched his arm. It was thick and corded, not like the soft white arm of her father who was a lawyer. "You're real."

"Yeah, I'm real and you're not stoned. What's wrong with you?"

She backed away again clutching the plastic bag. "I don't know what you're talking about."

"Your eyes, doll, you're not bombed, stoned, high on drugs, you're not sedated."

Then she understood. "I can't eat corn. It gives me bumps."

The larger boy who said his name was Logan laughed and elbowed his smaller friend. "She's gotta be the one person topside besides the doctor that ain't zonked. How funny is that?" He turned back to her and she noticed his blue eyes were clear, his gaze sharply assessing, and he was laughing at her because she was different.

"It's not my fault."

And then he smiled and she noticed how white his teeth were. He even had big eye teeth and two crooked ones on the bottom. Everyone she knew had perfect, white, dental implants or veneers.

"I'm allergic."

"So you can't take the drug. Your life must be really weird."

She shrugged. "They try to give me pills. I don't like them."

The entire population was addicted to a drug called Sopore. Sopore was a sedative genetically bred into corn by the chemical giant Monsonta. Corn, corn syrup, corn flour, corn starch, corn everything was in all the food. Shayna couldn't eat it so she had to eat special food her mother bought. Her parents tried to feed her the pills prescribed by her doctor to make her like everyone else, but she didn't like the way they made her feel, so she spit them out when no one was looking.

Logan smiled. "I'm not laughing at you," he said. "I'm just laughing because you and the Doc are probably the only two people topside that are straight."

She shrugged and made a face. "Yeah, Doctor Bob is like me. Maybe that's why I like working for him so much."

He stuck his hand out to her. He was wearing leather gloves with the fingers cut out. His younger friend huddled behind him, dark eyes wide in a terrified dark-skinned face. "What's your name?"

She took his hand. The feel of the leather was strange and his fingers were rough and calloused. "I'm Shayna."

"Well, Shayna, that bag you're hanging onto is for us. As soon as you hand it over, we gotta bounce."

She held it even tighter. "No, no, this is just trash. Doctor Wallace told me to put it in the red Dumpster."

Far in the distance, Shayna heard sirens. "There's an ambulance coming. I have to go."

The boy Logan tilted his head. "Ain't an ambulance, that's the Mole Patrol. They're coming for us. That frigging Sniffer." He pushed the younger boy. "Raj, run for the morgue."

He grabbed the bag of trash and turned to follow his friend who had taken off like a shot around the side of the building. The sirens were louder and there were a lot of them. Shayna's heart pounded. He was right. It wasn't an ambulance. She grabbed his arm. "No, don't go that way, they'll catch you. They're on the road behind the building. Come with me."

He pulled away from her, his blue eyes filled with terror. "I gotta go after Raj. They'll get him."

"There's no time. You have to come with me." The sirens were deafening. Shayna had never heard so many. Men began shouting and she heard the terrible singing of drones. Logan looked up at the same time as she did to see the unmanned helicopter diving toward them.

He dug in his heels when she tried to pull him along behind her. "Come on," she screamed.

"Raj!" Logan's call for the other boy was like the last scream of a dying man. He knew it was too late.

She tugged on his arm and he turned toward her with a look of pain and anguish contorting his features she'd never seen on anyone's face before. As they raced back into the ER, Shayna tried to think. Where could she hide him? She dragged him through back corridors usually traveled only by doctors. He was dressed in scrubs like all the nurses and doctors in the hospital and she had on her Candy Striper uniform. But his hair was too long and he had on those gloves. She pulled him into a closet, ripped through a pile of stacked garments and yanked out a surgical cap and a white doctor's jacket. "Put these on and keep your hands in your pockets."

She took the trash bag from him. "Doctors don't carry trash." They exchanged one long glance and then she opened the closet door, peered out and grabbed Logan's arm. "Come on."

They walked slowly but with purpose down a quiet, tiled hallway to a set of double doors. She turned and stuck her face close to his. He didn't smell bad, he just smelled different; earthy and warm. Being this close to him made her shiver, but not with fear. She should be afraid, but she wasn't. "Don't talk. Your speech patterns are wrong."

He nodded and she led him down a wide hallway between cubicles with curtains. A nurse ran by going the other way. She didn't seem to notice them. Shayna breathed a sigh of relief, opened one of the curtains and shoved Logan through in front of her. A huge man lay on the narrow bed. His fat hung off both sides. His enormous, flat, bare feet stuck out over the end of the bed. His eyes were encased in nests of blubber and they were closed.

"He drank too much soda," Shayna whispered. "Sopore overdose. They pumped his stomach. He'll probably sleep like the dead for hours."

She opened a closet door and shoved him inside. "They'll never look in here. I'll come back for you when it's clear." She handed him the white trash bag. "What's in it that's so important?"

"Medicine for my people." He took the bag and grabbed her hand. "What about my friend?"

"I don't know. I'll tell Doctor Wallace. Maybe he can find out what's going on. I'm just a Candy Striper. I volunteer."

He squeezed her hand. "Thanks."

VAGRANT

She pushed him into the closet. "I'll be back."

Logan tried to be patient and wait, but all he could think about was poor Raj. The kid was all alone with no chip in a strange world with strict rules he didn't understand. He had to find him before he got snatched and shipped off world. He inched the door open and peered into the cubicle. Snores loud enough to suck in the curtains echoed through the room. The man on the bed had consumed too much soda, and overdosed on the drug in the corn. How often did this happen? Thank goodness the people he knew, the mole people, the Vagrants, his people, grew their own food and rarely had the opportunity to eat food with the drug in it.

Once out of the closet, Logan shoved the trash bag into his empty pack and hid it under the white physician's coat as he slipped into the hallway and began making his way toward the lobby and the elevators. He saw flashing lights through huge windows in the lobby and stopped in front of the door to the stairwell to watch. Everyone in the lobby pressed against the windows watching the drama unfold. Uniformed Enforcers wearing body armor, black uniforms with the bright orange patches of the super city New Washington, loaded with weapons, were everywhere. He caught a glimpse of Raj being hustled between two huge Enforcers and felt his heart drop. They had him. *Poor Raj*. The Enforcers shoved his little buddy into the back of a black hovercraft. The hovercraft lifted and shot away carrying Raj off to a containment center.

Logan entered the stairwell and went down to the bottom floor. He had no desire to go back down the morgue drain. There were other ways into his world. He walked down the dark hallway seeing no one and stopped at the door to the incinerator. He glanced both ways and then ducked into the room where trash and the unclaimed dead were burned. The huge furnace filled the room. It was off. They burned on a strict schedule. Barrels of trash and one body waited. The furnace would be cranked up in an hour. The custodian in charge of the incinerator was walking the hospital right now making sure he had all contaminated waste gathered in this room to burn.

He opened the door to the furnace, climbed inside and shut it behind him. On the back side was the ash door. He opened it and went through into a small space filled with fine ash. When he kicked it aside, he found the cover to the hole into the sewers. He lifted it, slid into the dark and dropped onto a ledge. Ash weighted with the eternal fog of steam turned to a gray mud. He plowed through it and dropped to the walkway along the river of sewage. He barely noticed the stink as he headed down ten more levels deep under the city. He breathed a sigh of relief when he popped out of a passage into the huge open cavern of Vagrant City.

Chapter Two

Shayna had gone to the lobby to watch the drama. She saw the Enforcers catch Logan's small friend and shove him into the black hovercraft. It wasn't fair. He hadn't been doing anything, but she knew why they took him. He didn't have a chip. He was a Vagrant.

Everyone in her world got a microchip implanted in their hip when they were born. It contained all their vital statistics in a barcode; their Social Security numbers, their place of birth, their parents, everything. Without a chip you were a nobody. You didn't exist, couldn't have a job, a bank account or walk down the street. There were scanners on streetlights that checked all people for their chips. When you went into any building through the front door, you walked through a scanner. With a chip, you didn't even need a key for your building or your house, the chip opened the doors. Somewhere there was an agency that could access your chip and program new data into it or take data out.

When the hovercraft lifted and flew away, she walked slowly back to the ER. Maybe the doctor could tell her where they'd taken the boy. Doctor Bob was in his office. It was late, time for her to go home. She knocked on the door of his small cubicle and he reached over and opened it with one hand. She edged inside and stared down at him. Confusion and strange anxiety filled her. She'd never felt like this before. Her world was so ordered and controlled.

"What's up, Shayna? You look like you've seen a ghost."

She shook her head. "I'm sorry, Doctor Bob, I'm just confused. I met this guy named Logan. He came for the trash. He came from down there." Her last sentence was whispered and she pointed to the floor.

Doctor Bob reached behind her and shut the door. The office was smaller than a storage closet. The desk and two file cabinets about filled it. There was one metal chair in front of the desk. She turned it sideways and sat down.

"What did he tell you?"

"There were two of them. The Enforcers took his friend away. He told me the trash was really medicine for his people. Is that what you do? Help them?"

Doctor Bob leaned back in his chair and closed his eyes. "You know you're different, don't you?"

"I can't eat stuff with corn in it."

He nodded. "There's an entire population of people living below us in the old subway tunnels and even further below in subterranean caverns and the sewers. They don't have chips and it's hard for them to survive. I try to help. There's kids down there, babies, old people."

"Why did they take his friend away? He was just a boy."

"They'll send him off world to the mines. They discover more and more planets every day. They need people to settle them. They only want people who have chips and who are on the drug. The drug keeps the peace. It keeps everyone happy. There's no need for law enforcement unless a Vagrant comes up from down below. None of the people on the drug question the authority. That's why they keep trying to make you take the pills."

Shayna reached into the pocket of her red-striped apron and touched the two pills her mother had handed her early that morning. She pulled them out and showed them to the doctor. "I hate feeling like that. It's like walking around in a fog."

"Well you're about alone. I won't eat anything I know has Sopore in it so I stay straight, but it's in almost everything. Even the meat is filled with it because they feed corn to cows, chickens and pigs. It's addictive. Once you get started on it, getting off is horrible." He made a face. "I know."

"I thought the boy I talked to was nice. His eyes were so clear and he was so alert and vibrant."

"Forget about him, Shayna, and forget about the one they hauled away. You'll never see either of them again."

"Won't Logan come back for more medicine?"

"I'll tell them to send someone else. It's too dangerous for you to know him. Talking to any of them will taint you. The Company will find out and you'll be forced to take the drug or they'll ship you off with the Vagrants. Everyone does what they're told in this world, Shayna. Rebellion of any kind is out of the question. They have cameras and Ears everywhere. I love this small office. I could have a bigger one, but they'd put devices in it to watch me. This is the one place on the planet where I feel safe. Now go home and forget about that boy and the Vagrants and the world underground."

Shayna nodded. Her mind was spinning. It was as though she'd just woken up from a dream and been told everything she knew or believed in was false. She handed her uniform to her boss, Mrs. Cramer, an older woman with pink hair, a lot of makeup and that glassy-eyed stare.

Mrs. Cramer patted her arm. "You do such a good job, Shayna. Dr. Wallace always gives you great reviews." She pointed to a huge calendar on the wall behind her desk. "It looks like you come back in on Thursday. I'll see you then."

Shayna nodded. A thirty-two ounce soda sat on Mrs. Cramer's desk and Shayna wondered if the woman knew what she was drinking. Probably not.

Shayna's home was in a new high rise in Harlem. Most of Harlem was brand new, shiny stainless-steel structures with lots of glass. Her parents had told her Harlem used to be government housing and slums. There were still small stores sandwiched between the high rises, grocery stores, markets, robot-operated fast-food restaurants, but the city was squeaky clean.

Her father was a lawyer. He worked downtown for the Company. Her mother was a CPA with an office on Wall Street. The two of them made plenty of money and could afford the best of everything. Shayna rarely saw either of them.

She took the A train home, walking through the turnstile without slowing down. Her chip and her credit disk were all she needed. It was something she never worried about. The subway was clean and only registered members of society rode it. While she waited for the train, she stared into the darkness of the tunnel and thought about Logan. She thought she saw movement deep in the dark, then the train's headlight swept around a corner and it was gone.

There was no one at the door to her apartment building. Her parents had told her about the days of the New York doorman. No doorman was needed since no one could enter the building without a chip. No one could go into the elevator without a chip. It would let an undocumented Vagrant in, but then it would lock down until the Enforcers came to open it and extract the Vagrant. For the first time in her life, she wondered where they went when they were captured, what happened to them, what was their fate?

Their apartment was on the sixteenth floor. The elevator zipped up there so fast, she felt breathless when she walked out. She'd never get used to that feeling. The apartment door slid open when she approached it. A voice deep inside the four-bedroom unit greeted her. "Good afternoon, Miss Nagata. How was your day?"

"Fine," Shayna answered, though why she felt the need to talk to a computer was beyond comprehension.

She walked into the stainless-steel kitchen unit and smacked the door of the small fridge with her open palm. It opened to reveal a complete corn-free meal on a tray, everything wrapped in cellophane. She looked at the meal and wrinkled her nose. Soy meat with soy gravy, a salad and a piece of plain white bread lay next to the fake meat. Where did her mother find bread with no corn syrup?

The rest of the refrigerator contained fruit, plain yogurt and lunch meat for her dad who lived off sandwiches. All cooked meals were delivered by the apartment complex through a servo unit built into the wall. She, of course, could not eat them. The only other appliance in the kitchen was a small microwave. It had been installed because of her.

When she walked into the living room munching on her slice of bread, the sixty-inch holographic TV screen built into the wall flicked on to Fox News. "Miss Nagata, you should not be eating in the living area," the computer voice said.

Shayna shot a bird at the wall and gasped. Why had she done that? Had such a short encounter with Vagrants infected her with some kind of disrespectful bug, or maybe it had always been there lying in wait for the trigger that would set it off.

Still munching her bread, she sat on her mother's choice of furniture, a sleek, ultra-modern couch, switched the Holo's menu on, selected the internet option listed on the screen and accessed her Head Space account. Maybe she could find some information online about the Vagrants, information her parents had never given her. Her curiosity about them had been awakened by Logan. He was a real person, not a demon, not a boogie man to scare small children. So what else had her parents lied to her about?

Logan walked through a tunnel deep beneath the super city. It was lit with luminescent fungus grown in vats and then painted on the ceilings and walls inside all the living areas of the underground. The fungus lived off moisture from the damp atmosphere and nutrients found in the rocks. The tiny plants gave off a blue glow Logan found comforting. He turned down a narrow corridor lined with doors made from all kinds of materials. Some were mere curtains. Some were solid doors of wood. At the end of the corridor a door made of deep blue metal was shut and locked. It was the rear door of an old subway car.

The Professor lived in five old subway trains. The first one was his lab. The second and third were filled with hydroponic tanks where the Professor grew herbs and medicinal plants. The last two cars were living quarters. Logan paused for a moment, inhaled deeply, knocked three times, waited and knocked twice. The door flew open.

"Logan, glad to see you, man." Enoch Loughlin, better known as Knock, Logan's best friend, grabbed his hand and drew him into a chest bump. "How'd it go?"

Logan held out the bag. "Got the goods, but I lost Raj. I gotta go back and get him."

Professor Depak Goswami stepped out from behind a table filled with banks of test tubes, a huge electron microscope and two Bunsen burners. He flipped black goggles up and raised heavy eyebrows. "Raj was captured? How could you allow this to happen? He is my sister's nephew twice removed. What will I tell my wife? She will be most distressed."

"I'm so sorry, Professor. A Sniffer picked us up in Harlem. We'd just come out of the tunnel under the A line. We had to take the sewers. I thought I lost 'em, but they must have tracked us to the hospital. The Enforcers showed up like two minutes after we made the pickup site." Logan tossed the doctor the white trash bag. "I got the goods, but Raj got nailed. I'll go after him, Professor, you can count on me. I'll get him back."

The professor held the bag for a moment while he stared at Logan. "I think going topside on such a mission would be very foolhardy. I know you regret losing the boy to the Enforcers as do I, but you should not further risk yourself. You are too important to the people who need this medicine. You are the only runner we have who can get in and out of the hospital successfully."

The Professor opened the bag and pulled out boxes containing pills and bottles of medicine. He examined each one. When he pulled out a box of vials he sighed with relief. "Thank goodness we got the insulin. I have two patients in desperate need." He glanced at Logan. "Next time I will need more Sopore detox. Too many people are coming into our world addicted to that awful drug."

Logan nodded. "It's hard to get. They don't want people coming off it. They want them addicted."

Thinking about Sopore made him remember the girl with the dark hair. She wasn't addicted. He wondered what she was doing. He wished he could see her again and maybe talk to her over tea, or go for a walk along the river, but it was out of the question. Vagrants didn't have tea with legitimate citizens. He couldn't walk outside at all. He didn't have a chip. He'd be picked up as soon as he passed a scanner.

Knock drew him aside. "What happened, dude? Poor Raj, he's just a kid."

"I'm going back for him, Knock. I can't let them send him to a mining camp."

"The Professor thinks it's a bad idea, man. Too risky."

Logan shook his head. "It's my fault he's locked up. I should have been more careful. I knew it was his first time. I knew he was a greenie."

Knock put a hand on his shoulder. "If you feel you gotta go, then I'll go with you. You know I'm good."

"You are. This wouldn'ta happened if you'd been with me. The kid was too slow. He didn't even know how to chimney climb. I thought he'd had some training and could hang with me. I was wrong and that cost him everything."

Knock sat down on a massive lumpy sofa that might have been brown a long time ago. It and an overstuffed chair were pushed against the wall of the train. He reached down and picked up his board. Enoch was a skater. His board was the newest design of boards powered by electromagnetic systems. He'd invented the power pack himself and adapted it to a Free Ride hover board. It went faster and the pack's battery lasted forever because it was constantly recharging off the power lines of the subway. A picture of a spacecraft taking off from Kennedy Space Port was laminated to the bottom. The top was covered with a sheet of bumpy, gravel-coated material to give Enoch traction. He turned the board over and stroked the laminated space ship.

"Where'd they take him?"

"Don't know. Tomorrow, I'm gonna visit Eddie and get some equipment. Then I'm gonna get him to use his Kray to hack into the Company's records and find out where Raj is. We gotta get him before they hook up the Lift again and shoot him to the moon."

"When does that go down?"

"Don't know, maybe the Professor does. Hey Prof, when's the Lift go online again?"

Professor Goswami turned his skinny brown wrist over and checked his bulky watch. "The moon is within range beginning tomorrow. It will be full in three days and then there will be five more days the Lift will be able to operate."

"Crap!" Logan shot to his feet. "I'm gonna crash. We need to get out of here early." He stopped and stared at Knock. "That's if you still wanna go."

"You're kidding, right?"

Logan grinned. "Of course."

Chapter Three

Logan crept down the subway tunnel of the 6th Avenue Express. He could feel the electromagnetic field from the rail. The air shivered with energy. "Hurry," he shot over his shoulder. "I can feel a train coming."

The door to the neighboring tunnel for the A-Train was ten feet in front of him. He spotted it, leaped onto the ledge and put his *key* against the door. The special level-three key was a circular disc provided by Eddie Chou, a tech genius, to open all the subway access doors. Without it, the tunnel rats would be unable to move between the tunnels or access control rooms and get into the high speed rail system. These tubes were their super highways and the key was their ticket inside. Logan wore his on a leather cord around his neck.

Eddie had stolen one and managed to duplicate it. He sold them to the tunnel rats at an exorbitant price. Eddie said there were seven levels of keys. If you had a level-five key, you could go anywhere but the CEO's tower, even the Lift opened for a level-five key.

Inside the A-Train tunnel, Logan led them along the floor beside the single wide rail. They took off running. You never knew when to expect a train. He could always feel the energy emitted by the rail. His sensitivity had saved him from being killed by a train many times. A dog-size rat sat on a ledge on the other side of the rail. Enoch pointed. "Want me to bag it?"

"Sure," Logan whispered.

Knock pulled a blowgun out of his backpack, put it to his mouth and nailed the rat. Then he leaped on his magnetic skateboard, shot across the rail, scooped up the big animal by its naked tail, leaped into the air to reverse his direction and shot back to Logan. "Yo, this is the biggest one I've ever killed."

"They're getting bigger all the time. The Professor will have to treat it before we can eat it. It's probably full of Sopore. It didn't even move when it saw us."

"Stoned, man, seriously whacked."

Knock stowed his board and the rat in his pack while they walked. When they reached the access, Logan opened a metal door leading out of the A-Train tunnel, then they went down. Sometimes underground, you had to go down to get up. Logan opened a door with steps leading down to a crawl space under the rail system. It was supposed to be for maintenance personnel only and was bugged with Ears and Sniffers. The Company knew the mole people and the tunnel rats used the crawl space and this was where most of them got caught.

Logan's heart raced with adrenaline. The danger was something he fed off. He needed to feel the rush of fear running the tunnels gave him. It made him forget he was a Vagrant, a nobody whose father had been sent off world to work in the mines on lousy Gliese 667. It made him feel free. In the tunnels, Logan was a king. He'd been running them for ten years and knew every crawl space, every inch of the sewer and every exit to topside. Nobody, no Vagrant or tunnel rat knew the underground system like he did.

They silently inched through the crawl space passing three Ears blinking green in the darkness. They came to a manhole leading even further down. Logan rolled it open with a clank alerting one of the Ears which immediately blinked red. Logan pointed to it and Knock nodded. Somewhere topside, a computer had just alerted an Enforcer to their presence. It didn't matter. In a few seconds they'd be in the sewers.

VAGRANT

They dropped through the manhole, slid the cover into place and stood on a ledge overlooking a river. This wasn't like the sewer under the hospital. This was a rushing flood of water, an underground river filled with overflow from the Hudson, runoff coming into the system through street drains and water from the aqueducts that provided fresh water to the city. Logan loved this section of the sewer. Moisture filled the air from spray as the water raced and tumbled on its way to the East River. In this one giant sewer pipe, there were no Sniffers or Ears. They were safe. The dampness wrecked the inner workings of the robots and the sound of the water drowned out all other noise.

Logan turned to his friend and grinned. He held his arms out wide and breathed the ultra-fresh air and yelled. "I love it here, don't you?"

Enoch rolled his eyes and shook his head. "Why you going after this kid, Logan? He's just another tunnel rat. Once the Company has one . . . well no one has ever brought one back. So why?"

Logan shrugged. "This is the first time I lost one. I'm not like all the other runners. I've never lost a kid before, never, and this ain't gonna be on me. I'm gonna show everyone, you can beat the Company. I'm gonna get him back."

"Why bother man?" Knock asked as they edged along the river. "He's probably better off on some other planet, breathing the air of a free man, looking at the sky every day instead of the top of a tunnel six inches over his frigging head. What's the difference between him running the sewers and digging gold or uranium or diamonds on some other world? He'll have a chance, Logan, a chance for a different life."

Logan laughed. "That's about the most I ever heard you say before, Knock. Maybe I want to try to get him back to see if I can. Maybe it's a challenge I can't resist. I been thinkin' about going up against the Company for a long time."

"You got a death wish?"

Logan turned away and marched faster. "Not really, I think I'm just realizing I want something else out of life and if I'm gonna get it, I'm gonna have to fight."

They continued walking down the ledge above the river slowly because it was slippery with algae. Logan spotted a tube in the brick ceiling over their heads leading topside. It was high above the water and the landmark he'd been looking for. He stopped on the ledge and searched for the entrance to Eddie Chou's high-tech workshop. It was a shimmering spot on the wall, impossible to find if you didn't know where to look. Chou had created a device that altered light and made the door invisible. Logan touched a spot in the middle of the shimmering bricks and was immediately sucked through. Enoch followed and they emerged into an airlock.

Chou's lab was air conditioned and germ free. Hundreds of jets of air sprayed them down. The smell of some kind of antiseptic filled the air. A door much like a port on a space ship was in front of them. There was a double-paned window in it. A bearded face appeared in the window and the door opened with a sucking sound.

A skinny Asian man greeted them by waving without looking up from a Sniffer Hound lying dead on the table with its guts displayed. That was Eddie. The guy who opened the door grabbed Logan and pulled him into the room. Logan had never seen him before. He was pasty white, dumpy, wore thick glasses with ear pieces that plugged directly into his ears, and an unfocused gaze. The glasses had him plugged directly into Chou's matrix.

Huge hi-def and holographic screens lined the walls, some with green words scrolling endlessly down a black background; some obviously interfacing with the Company's computers displayed various spots in the city. On one, hundreds of topside workers sat at desks with banks of screens on each desk. Logan pointed to that one. "Where's that?" Logan asked the dumpy guy.

Startled, the man pushed the glasses up. "Huh?"

"Where is that?"

"That, my friend, is the center of the universe, the main control room for the Company. Everything is run from about a hundred rooms just like that in the central tower downtown."

A chill of fear ran up Logan's spine. He'd always known Eddie was crazy, but tapping into the Company's systems to watch them was seriously deviant behavior. But that was why he was here. If he was going to save Raj, he needed to know where they were holding him and the only person he knew who could find out stuff like that was Eddie.

"What's your name?" he asked the dumpy guy.

"Humphrey, but everyone calls me Hump."

"I'm Logan. Cool glasses. What do they do?"

Hump took them off and passed them to Logan. When he put them on, he gasped. "It's like I'm inside the computer. I can move anywhere just by using my eyes." He took them off and examined them. "How do they work?"

"New technology allows you to interface with your brainwaves and ocular movement. You should try playing Medal of Honor with them. It's like you're there on another planet fighting aliens. It's so real."

Logan couldn't see anything particularly different about the glasses aside from the thick rims and earpieces. "How can you wear them and walk?"

"Just click them off, man, it's easy. When you need them, think on, and they boot up."

****

Deklan Hall carried one skinny old woman on his back and held another under his arm like a sack of flour as they climbed the mountain of slag piled up outside the mine. Two men and two other women slogged up the mountain behind him each carrying a pack of supplies and equipment. He'd had enough of mining for the Company. He had the training to fight a war all by himself if he wanted to, but these people needed him and wanted to go. They were breaking for freedom and a new life on this crazy planet.

At the top of slag mountain he stopped and put the emaciated woman down. She wobbled for a minute and one of the men stepped forward and handed her a walking stick made from a shovel handle. Deklan hitched his plates up and tightened the belt holding them in place. He carried an M-32p5, the newest high-powered, fully automatic rifle available in the world. Its previous owner was currently resting for eternity in an abandoned mine shaft. Belts of ammo wrapped around his waist and his old friend, a Marine K-Bar knife, was tight to his chest in its worn sheath. The Company might have arrested him and brought him here, but they didn't have what it took to keep him a prisoner.

The landscape spread out before them was awe-inspiring and incredible. Gliese 667 was smaller than earth with a lighter field of gravity. Deklan was Superman here, able to leap tall slag heaps in a single bound and carry two women with him. On the plain at the base of the mountain, a blue-green river cut through auburn grass.

Deklan lifted his field glasses and spotted a herd of jumping jacks, the local term for an indigenous life form that ate the grass and hopped like rabbits. They were the size of a deer and rumored to taste pretty good. After a diet of soy protein and fungus grown in underground vats, Deklan yearned for his first taste of a jumper.

A ten-foot high razor wire fence ran around the mining camp. The only way over it was the crumbling, mountainous slag heap which was virtually impossible to climb unless you were desperate. The heap was made of sharp red lava rock, shiny black shards of obsidian and hematite and tiny sharp pieces of a natural material the Company called gliesite after the planet. Pieces of gliesite broke into barbs and crumbled easily. The two men with him wore their mining clothes under stolen Company uniforms made of Kevlar. If they hadn't worn the Kevlar they'd all have been cut to pieces.

The two women climbing beside them were wrapped in jumper-leather garments they'd made themselves. They all wore jumper-hide gloves. Company men hunted the herbivores for sport, ate the backstrap and the haunches and threw the rest away along with the hides which was typical of the wasteful, sadistic jerks.

They slid down the far side of the slag heap, Deklan once again carrying the two older women, and stopped to get their bearings before setting off toward the river. Water on Gliese was rare, but he'd heard this one river ran for miles through the plains and barren land before it eventually dumped into a small fresh-water sea. He wanted to get as far away from the mine as possible before the mining commander, Colonel Randal Cummings, discovered they were gone and sent a helo to search for them. They were only a small group, seven. Deklan had heard the Colonel only sent out a helo for ten or more escapees. If that kind of rule was in place, Deklan figured there were more people out here and the best way to find them was to follow the river.

Deklan put the old woman down and handed her the stick. He looked back the way they'd come and saw the sun beginning to set. The Gliese 667 star system had four suns. The closest one to their planet was a red dwarf, Gliese 667 C. The official designation of the planet they were on was GJ 667 Cc. It had been discovered in the early part of the twenty-first century and settled in 2026 when an exploratory expedition discovered diamonds the size of birds' eggs and other gemstones in the volcanic substrata. The Company set up the mining camp ten years later and had been pulling mega money off the planet ever since. Deklan didn't give a crap about the profits of the Company. He wanted to breathe free air and he had the skills necessary to make it out here.

One of the men, Tom Curran, walked up beside him. Deklan thrust out his chin and waved. "Take the point, I'll guard the rear."

"Will do, Sergeant," Curran said.

Everyone here knew he'd been a Sergeant in the Rangers. They knew he'd been injured, got out after the Afghanistan war ended and never quite fit into civilian life. They respected him which was a good thing. Deklan would put anyone down who endangered this mission. Freedom was on the horizon and Deklan was marching for it.

The old woman's name was Maria Rodriguez. She dropped back to talk. Deklan had allowed her to come because of all the members of this group she was the only one who had been out here before. She knew what was edible and what wasn't and had a reputation as a witch. She'd recruited the other members and vouched for their skills and determination.

VAGRANT

"When I was out here before," she said. "I was just a young girl. But I remember a lot. There are creatures in the river we can eat, but we have to be careful, there are also predators in the deeper sections."

Deck grinned. "I don't care about predators, Maria, all I care about is getting us as far away from the camp as possible. I'm not going back. If I die, at least it will be breathing free air."

"Do you ever think about your boy?"

Deklan's smile faded. "Do you think about yours?"

She dropped her head, pulling a rough scarf made from feed sacks over her graying hair. "My son is dead to me. He forced me to return to the camp and then joined the Company. There is no room in my heart for such a traitor. He preferred captivity to a life of freedom in the wilds."

"I miss my kid, but I taught him a lot before I was captured. He's a tough nut and he'll survive."

"Think you will ever see him again?"

Deklan shook his head. "I hope not because that would mean he was here on Planet Hell and a Company prisoner. I like to think of him as free, well as free as anyone can be under the thumb of the Company."

Chapter Four

Logan scanned the screen in front of him for Raj's name. Eddie had located the list of prisoners in the Company's system, but it was unbelievably long. The green names against the black background scrolled by as Logan searched. He finally realized they were listed by the date of arrest not alphabetically and scrolled back up.

When he found Rajesh Kumaran, his stomach fell like a stone. Raj was already on the moon. They'd shipped off a load of prisoners that very morning on the Lift.

He pushed his chair away from the wooden table with the banks of screens and rubbed a gloved hand over his eyes. What was he supposed to do now? Give up? Forget it? Let the Company win?

Knock kicked the back of his chair. "What's wrong, dude? You look like you're gonna hurl."

"They already shipped him to the moon." Logan pointed to a green name. "See, says right here sent to the O'Reilly Holding Center on Moon Base Alpha for shipment to the Lyra system and Kepler 62f on the next cargo flight."

"Is that where they sent your dad?"

Logan's turned away from Enoch's searching stare. "No, he's on the hell planet in the Gliese system."

"You loved your dad, didn't you?"

"Yeah, I loved him. But he's gone. What am I supposed to do? He told me to soldier on if he ever got caught, and that's exactly what I been doing."

Knock smacked the back of his head. "Hey, at least you know who your dad is."

33

"Don't mess with me, Knock, you still got a mom."

"Sure I do, a mom who's so messed up on Sopore, she forgets to eat or where she is half the time."

Logan stood up and shoved the rolling chair toward the airlock. "So, want to take a ride on the Lift? All I need is a Level-Five key."

Knock's eyes rounded. "Uh, no, you wanna die? And where you gonna get a Level Five? I ain't even seen one and I don't know anybody who's seen one."

"I want to get Raj back and I don't give up . . . ever. Hey Eddie, has anyone ever gone to the moon and come back?"

Eddie did something with a soldering iron to the insides of the Sniffer. Sparks flew and Eddie laughed. "This is gonna be fun."

Logan looked over Eddie's shoulder. "What did you do to it?"

"I turned it into a bomb. The next person that opens this Sniffer's chest, is gonna explode along with anything within a twenty-foot radius."

Logan nodded his head. "Now that is cool, but you didn't answer my question. Is it possible to go to the moon, snatch a prisoner and get back here in one piece?"

Eddie's face contorted into a mass of wrinkles as he laughed. His slanted eyes disappeared into folds of sagging yellow flesh. "You gotta be kidding. You can't go to the moon on the Lift, Loge. It ain't possible. You'll die or get shipped off world with the rest of the pick-ups. There's guards at both ends, there's security up the ying yang. It's impossible."

"Is there any other way to get up there besides the Lift?"

Eddie rolled his eyes. "You don't take no well, do you? The only other way to the moon is on a rogue space ship operated by the Tong. The Dragon Tong has the smuggling racket wrapped up.

They got the only ships allowed off world by the Company. They run a small base on the dark side of the moon and they pay for the privilege. They would expect you to pay as well. That's how they make their money."

Logan glanced at Enoch who shook his head vigorously. "Count me out. I ain't messing with the Tong. They're worse than the Company. They don't send you off world to mine, they eject you into space without a space suit."

Logan shrugged off Knock's negativity. "How do I contact the Tong?"

"You have money, a lot of money?" Eddie asked.

"I have something they might want I can swap for a ride."

Eddie made a face like he'd just sucked a lemon. "What?"

"Just set up a meet for me, will you?"

Eddie lifted one shoulder. "It's your funeral."

Logan poked the entrails of the inert Sniffer. "Can you make this thing so it goes off with a remote control?"

Eddie tilted his head and rolled his eyes. "Do rats leave a sinking ship?"

"I don't know," Logan said. "Never been on one. Are there rats on space ships?"

Eddie chuckled. "You know, there actually are. The one Tong guy I know, Leonard Ching, has a cat named Toad-Sticker, big orange Tom cat with no tail. He told me all the Chinese spacers have cats to keep down the rat population and catch any alien stowaways."

"That's disgusting. Knock, show Eddie the big sucker you caught in the subway today."

Enoch pulled the giant rat out of his pack and held it by the tail. "Nice one, eh?"

35

Eddie shook his head. "I'm thinking the ones on the space ships aren't that big."

"Pack it away Knock, you're making Eddie nervous. Hey, Eddie, can I borrow one of your chips?"

Logan had to go topside to collect the item he felt would buy his ticket to the moon and he couldn't walk a foot up there without a chip. Eddie had a contact at a funeral home that sold chips taken from dead bodies on the black market. This whole plan he was formulating in the back of his head was a long shot. His dad had taken him to a place when he was little and hidden something, something really valuable. With a few of Eddie's toys and a little luck he might just pull this off.

Eddie knelt down and reached into his safe. "Why do you need one all of a sudden? You're the king of the tunnel rats."

Logan smiled. "Everyone has their own little secrets. If what I'm planning works out, you'll get more than paid, you'll be rich."

Shayna was bored with the inane crap the Company put on all the viewing channels. She was bored with her online friends, bored with being alone all the time. All her friends were stoned on Sopore and about as exciting as leaf mold. She kept thinking about Logan and how interesting his life was. He lived under the city. How hard could he be to find?

The thought of going underground made her stomach roll and her face hot. She grabbed her cheeks. What was she thinking? Did she want some excitement in her life or did she want to see Logan again? As she grabbed her hat and coat off the hook by the door, she smiled. It was a little of both.

When she got to the door, she stopped. "Open."

The door did not move.

"You may not egress, Ms. Negata," the home computer said. "You are supposed to stay on the premises. Your parents programmed me with explicit instructions to ensure that you did."

Shayna walked to the apartment's main com panel hidden in a small compartment in the kitchen and switched the computer control system off. She swept a low bow with her hat in her hand to the now dead computer. "I'll be leaving now."

Once out the door and in the hallway, Shayna's courage almost failed. When her parents came home and found the apartment's controls turned off, they would freak. She stopped at the elevator. It sensed her chip and opened for her. "Ground floor," she said and the bottom dropped out from beneath her feet.

She walked out of the elevator with the familiar feeling of shame and relief she always felt. She'd been riding in the high-speed lifts her entire life. They were modeled after the big Lift that connected Earth to the moon fifteen nights of the month. Now that was a ride she never wanted to take.

When she was out of the building and on the street, she stopped to stare up at her apartment. The building rose high into the city sky, a blazing beacon of stainless steel and glass aglow in the late afternoon sun. Filled with determination, she strode toward the tunnel entrance on 125th Street. That subway line intersected with the Loop that shot all the way to Boston one way and south to Richmond the other way. The Loop ran side by side with the B line and the C and E local lines. It was a huge underground station. She reasoned that would be where the tunnel runners could be found. If she saw one, she intended to ask about Logan.

She crammed her hands in her pockets and hunched her shoulders against the light drizzle. All around neon lights blinked, people of all races and ethnicities crowded the streets walking slowly, their faces stuck in the Sopore stare. That's what Shayna called it. Her parents got it all the time. They'd just sit and look at the stupid stuff on the holo screen like they were in a trance.

She saw the occasional hover taxi shoot by overhead but most of the city's residents rode on the subway. It was easy, safe and went everywhere. She hit the stairs descending into the tunnel surrounded by a crowd. They didn't run or hurry, they walked steadily like robots, all moving at the same pace. There was little conversation among them making the descent into the subway system eerily quiet. When she passed them, they didn't even look at her.

Inside the well-lit station, she moved toward the empty track with her heart pounding. Maybe this wasn't that great of an idea. Then she remembered the flickering shadows she'd seen in the subway tunnel when she'd last ridden it and pushed through the milling crowd waiting for the next train.

She took a ramp that lead up and over the C and E local line and walked down into the Loop. A giant tunnel made of Plexiglas disappeared into the dark in two directions. There was a small space on each side of the tube. She thought she could easily fit into it. Another ramp led over the Loop into the subway tunnel for the 6th Avenue Express. She looked both ways, saw the people waiting for the Loop standing quietly, staring at nothing, and slipped into the space next to the Plexiglas tube.

The Loop's tunnel was dimly illuminated by overhead lights placed at twelve-foot intervals. She walked quickly, concentrating on her footing. Huge pieces of gravel lined the tunnel floor making it rough to walk. She wore soft-soled boots suitable for the city not this and she was afraid she'd fall. When she went around a corner, the station disappeared and she was alone. Her heart began racing as she thought about the mole people. Logan had said they were just normal humans like her, but suddenly she was assailed with doubt.

A metal door appeared in the tunnel wall. There was no handle. She touched it and nothing happened. The Loop began humming. The hum turned to an ear-splitting whine and she covered her ears. The Plexiglas vibrated. She could feel energy coming off it. The high-speed train shot into view, its headlamp briefly illuminated her. An unearthly screech forced her against the wall with its ferocity. The train was braking.

"Open!" She screamed at the door. It slowly slid open and she fell into the black space inside with relief. The door slid shut behind her.

The tiny space was filled with huge, metal electronics boxes stamped with the Company logo, a yellow atom in the center of three red circles. Above her a yellow light bulb inside a cage filled the small room with bile-colored light. She saw a large circle of metal in the floor and a tiny access door in the back wall. She reasoned the door would lead into the subway line she'd crossed. The only way into the world of the Vagrants was through the circular opening.

She knelt down and touched the metal circle. It was like a manhole in the street, dark gray and bumpy with the logo of the Company embossed on the center. She pushed it and nothing happened. She ordered it to open like she had the door and it slowly slid counterclockwise, clanking loudly when it stopped. Everything was programmed to read her chip. Somewhere, in some room, a computer had registered her chip down here. She briefly wondered if that was a bad thing.

When she looked through the hole in the floor, she saw a ladder leading down into terrible darkness. She touched an icon on her wrist com and a holographic display appeared in front of her. She selected the app icon, and clicked on the flashlight. Her wrist com lit up with a bright light in a pencil beam. She shined it into the darkness. The tunnel leading down seemed to go on forever. A damp, fetid smell with astringent overtones drifted out of the hole. It reminded her of a chemical toilet. Did this hole lead to the sewer?

She sat down heavily, put her head in her hands and squeezed. Tears filled her eyes. She had yet to see even one Vagrant or tunnel runner and no mole people, not that she'd recognize one if she saw one, and the underground system seemed enormous, way bigger than she'd imagined. Somehow she'd thought she'd find a big cavern filled with happy, warm people like Logan. This was not like that at all.

.

Chapter Five

When Deklan stepped off the slag heap and into the grass, he realized it wasn't the color of weak tea. It was actually many strands of different colored grass waving in the slight breeze. He looked down and saw red, yellow, blue and green strands twining together as though alive. He stepped onto free ground for the first time in ten years. He'd spent five underground with Logan and the last five working in the mines. Laboring in the Company's employ had made him strong. When he flexed his biceps they were huge, his old Ranger tattoo, a skull with Ranger running through it, bulged.

Taking the point, Curran headed toward the river followed by a young guy named Terrance McGee. McGee was only nineteen, his hair a fiery red, ginger beard on a pointed chin and arched brows over moss green eyes giving him the look of an Earth fox. The two women, Maria and Declan's woman, Mai Li, followed McGee, another ex-Ranger named Cain Hollyroad, followed the women, then two girls, both Mai Li's daughters born here on Gliese, Ju and Fenfang, walked behind Hollyroad. Deklan walked fifteen paces behind panning the wide open plain with his rifle.

All Dek's senses were on high alert. He hadn't been in the field in a lot of years, but it's not something you forget. They neared the river and Maria called to Curran to stop. They all gathered around her. "There is quicksand along the river. Many escapees have tried to get water from the river only to die a horrible death struggling in bottomless pits of sand."

Dek scanned the riverbank with his field glasses. "What's it look like?"

"Green," Maria said. "It looks like fine green grass you would feel safe to walk upon. When we get into that stand of korov trees, I will show Tom the safe path. We need to cross the river as soon as possible to put it between us and the mines."

Dek leaned close to her. "Are there other people out here, Maria? Do I need to watch for human attackers as well?"

She patted him, her hand small on his enormous forearm. "You watch for water monsters much like crocodiles laying in the sun and the spotted predators. They live in the trees and can snag you and drag you into the boughs before you realize they are there. Look for foliage that moves or seems to move. They are like chameleons and can disappear against leaves so well, you can't see them."

Maria led them into the shade of the trees. She pointed to a smooth patch of green which looked like it was covered with short green grass. "Quicksand," she whispered. "There is the path."

The path she indicated was little more than a jumper game trail. It threaded its way through the tall grass and the shadowy tree trunks. Dek was on high alert as Curran led the way along the game trail. On his left, the river, blue-green from the slag heap, appeared translucent up close. He saw the bottom, red lava rock mixed with black obsidian and gliesite. The occasional flash of silver indicated life forms in the water. He turned his attention back to the tree canopy and searched for Maria's spotted predators.

Mai dropped back to walk with him. They'd been together for a year, plotting and planning this break for freedom. She didn't want her girls sold to the miners. They were small for their age, but the looks had begun, the sly innuendos along with the leers, all indications their time as children was running out.

Mai breathed deeply. The air on Gliese had a higher concentration of oxygen than Earth. It gave humans extra stamina. Dek inhaled as well, savoring the scents of freedom. The mines had reeked of human waste and bad air. Out here, he smelled a spicy cinnamon-like odor blended with the moist scent of the wet earth beside the river and a tart smell that tickled the nose.

"What's the fruity smell, Maria?" He called to her.

She turned and looked at him. "Berries," she pointed. "They are good to eat. We will pick some when we camp."

"This is a good place," Mai said to him. "There is danger here, but there is danger in the mines. Out here, at least we are allowed to avoid it."

Dek put his big left hand on her shoulder and squeezed. "I wish Logan could be here. I think he'd like it."

****

Logan had Eddie's chip in his pocket, Hump's glasses on his face and his heart in his throat. He hadn't walked above ground, pretending like he belonged there, for over a year. Eddie was pretty stingy with his chips. They were hard to get, and Logan had no reason to be up here.

In the back of his mind, he searched for Shayna and wondered where she was and what she was doing. He'd look for her on his next hospital run. Right now, he needed to concentrate on his mission, find his father's stash spot and clean it out.

When his dad first came back from Afghanistan, he worked as a security guard for the Titan Construction Company. They were working on the Brooklyn Bridge which was now just a walking and bicycling bridge. There were few personal vehicles allowed in the cities, and most were hovercraft anyway, so there was no need for all the bridges. Everyone used the tunnels which had been rebuilt with state-of-the-art technology ten years ago. The Tube had its own tunnels and the trains had theirs. Most of the bridges had then been torn down. The older ones like the Brooklyn Bridge, High Bridge, the Third Avenue Bridge and the Williamsburg Bridge, the Company had saved as historic landmarks.

Logan remembered his dad working on the old bridge. He'd gone down to the park with him. The park was under the Brooklyn tower on the other side of the East River. You could walk right up to two of the supports. There was grass and a playground.

Security for Titan was the last job his dad had, the one he was on when he was fired and became unemployed in a city where the unemployed had no place.

They had taken a trip to the park late one night and his dad showed him a brick in the base of a support for the bridge. It was loose and his dad had pulled it out. Behind the loose brick was a space. His dad had picked him up so he could look inside. The space behind the brick was filled with a burlap sack. His dad had told him the bag held treasure and it would be their secret. He'd used mortar and refitted the brick.

With his chip and a credit disk supplied by Eddie, Logan actually rode the subway. He took the Lexington Avenue Express. Ten minutes into the ride, he got a very bad feeling. His shoulders itched and the hair on his neck rose. Someone was watching him!

Carefully, so as not to attract attention, he scanned the other people on his car. It only took a second to ID the man watching him. A special branch of the Enforcers, the Secret Service or SS, traveled through the cities undercover. Their idea of traveling undercover was to wear a black suit, black tie and dark, wrap-around sunglasses. Everyone knew what they looked like. A member of the SS leaned against the rear door of the train watching him.

Logan's heart pounded and he felt ready to hurl. What had he done to alert the SS? He mentally reviewed his clothes. They were a little worn and he was carrying a backpack. When he checked out the other travelers, he realized he was the youngest. School in the cities ran from eight in the morning until five. It was two. Crap! They thought he was playing hooky, which was a freaking crime. Your parents could be sent to the mines if your kid failed to attend school. The Company was actively looking for conscripts to work in the mines and the service colonies growing around them. They'd send you off world for spitting on the sidewalk.

His train slowed as it pulled into a stop on Prince Street. He did his best to pretend he wasn't interested. He had to swallow the huge lump in his throat as his heart raced. A woman carrying a shopping bag edged by him toward the exit as Logan leaned against a center pole and looked at the ceiling. The SS officer moved slowly in his direction. The doors opened with a hiss and Logan bolted, ran behind the train and into the tunnel. He heard pounding feet behind him and screams of annoyance as people were shoved aside.

"Stop or I'll shoot!" The SS officer called.

Logan didn't take the time to look behind him and he didn't stop. He saw the access door ahead, yelled "Open!" It slid aside thanks to his borrowed chip and he leaped into it.

Once inside the machinery room, Logan didn't stop. He needed to get to the bridge. There was a door on the other side. He opened it, looked into the Loop's tunnel and stepped onto the gravel. As the door shut behind him he heard the other door clang open. The SS officer was close behind.

Logan jogged beside the Plexiglas tube until he reached a spot in the wall covered with crazy Vagrant and mole people graffiti. A small tunnel had been dug under the Plexiglas. He glanced back, saw the door opening from the machinery room, dove into the shallow tunnel with his pack in front of him, and squirmed through it to the other side. Without slowing, he leapt to his feet, ran to the platform, climbed up and raced across the ramp over the Loop that led to the subway. He was just in time to leap through the door of the train he'd just jumped out of while it was closing. The train took off as the SS officer ran onto the platform.

He wasn't safe. The SS were wired together, each in constant connection with the other through those dark glasses. Logan moved swiftly through the train until he was in the last car. He took up a position against the rear door where he had a clear view of the passengers and a fast way to exit into the tunnels.

When the train slowed for the Canal Street stop, Logan opened the door and dropped into the tunnel. He made his way to the platform, slid into the crowd heading for the surface and tried to disappear. He saw two SS running down the escalator, pushing people aside rudely, and pressed his body between a fat woman carrying a briefcase and a huge shoulder bag and an old man wearing a wide-brimmed hat. The old man gave him a dirty look, but the fat woman gave him a dreamy smile. He grinned at her and she grinned back.

On the surface, he ran for a 101 Bus just pulling to the curb. Its wheels were down for the stop, he leapt aboard, his borrowed credit disk automatically being deducted for the fare when he walked by the scanner. A loud expulsion of air indicated the wheels of the bus were up. It rose into the air and shot down Third Avenue as Logan fell into an empty seat. He checked the passengers and didn't see any Enforcers. With a sigh, he leaned back, took some deep breaths and wiped beaded sweat off his forehead.

When they passed City Hall, he saw Enforcers and SS everywhere. They moved with a purpose toward the subway tunnel and their parked vehicles. Logan had no doubt he was the reason. He needed to get to the bridge, find his father's hidey hole and get back where he was safe . . . underground.

He got off the bus at Fulton Street. He looked half a block down, past a row of older buildings and busy shops, to the opening into the subway. The bus was much slower than the train. If the SS and the Enforcers were down there, they hadn't been able to guess where he'd gone or was going. He walked with a purpose, not too fast, not too slow, toward the bridge. He had to get to the other side. While he was on the bridge, he would be vulnerable. His only escape would be to jump off and that was a sure death.

He climbed the steps from the paved pathway to the bridge and walked out onto the refinished surface. There were tourists and small knots of people walking or staring down at the water. He had a moment of queasiness. The East River below and the sky above were so vast and the enormity of it was overwhelming. He forced his attention on his feet, the concrete beneath them, as he took one step at a time and crossed the bridge. He kept glancing behind to make sure he wasn't followed. When he was safely on the other side, he looked back and moaned. Two SS officers had just climbed the steps and were walking toward him. They separated, each one's mouths moving continuously as they kept contact with their fellow members, but they never looked directly at him.

He ran down steps into the park, stumbling on the last stair and falling onto the concrete. He ignored the stab of pain in his knee, leapt to his feet and raced off the path and onto the grass.

The green grass under his feet was soft, the earth spongy from the recent rain. The feel of it was so strange, Logan was momentarily distracted. A few people sat on blankets staring at the water. He saw a mother slowly pushing her child in a stroller, groups of tourists being regaled by guides, and a smattering of health-conscious joggers, but for the most part, the park was empty. It must be because it was a workday, everyone worked. Kids went into daycare and parents worked and older kids went to school all day. There were limits on how many children you could have. You had to apply for a permit and the Company based your allotted amount of children on several things such as income and heredity and of course, ethnicity.

He approached the bridge support cautiously, checking over his shoulder for the SS. He carried a backpack so he looked like a student, but students his age should be in school. He saw them coming down the steps into the park and groaned. This entire adventure had become dangerous. He should have done it at night.

Shrugging off the crazy feeling of déjà vu, he had been here before, and terror he'd be caught, he walked up to the support and examined the tan bricks. What would he do if he couldn't remember which one? They all looked alike. They all looked like they'd been there since the eighteen hundreds.

He tried to remember how high his dad had held him. He knew his dad was tall, almost six-four, and he had been six years old. He walked slowly around the support examining every brick. It took a while. After twenty minutes of checking each brick, he sat down on a bench and took some deep breaths. If he couldn't find his dad's stash, his entire plan would fail. On a hunch, he tapped the ear piece of his glasses and said, "Eddie."

The tech genius answered immediately. "Yo, this is Eddie."

"Eddie, I got a big problem."

"You've been picked up by the SS?"

Logan looked over his shoulder, his stomach knotting.

"They're after me, but I got away. How did you know?"

"We monitor their com band, duh. You led them a merry chase through the tunnels, but they're not gonna give up."

"Tell me something I don't know. Hey, I can't remember where my dad hid his stash. It's everything Eddie. I gotta find it."

"Treasure hunt, cool."

"No, not cool. I can't find the stash and I'm being hunted by the SS. Got any ideas?"

"There's an app for that on those glasses. If you scroll down, it says memory."

Logan scrolled through a long list of apps using his eyes to move the list along. "I see it. What's it do?"

"It taps into your memories. If you've been in a spot before, it will bring up the incident. You'll be able to relive the moment. It's pretty new. I invented it."

"This really works?"

"It should. Can't hurt to try."

"You're right. Thanks."

Chapter Six

Shayna slipped into the hole and climbed down into absolute dark. She used the light app on her watch to illuminate a tube covered with a slick green shiny coating that gave her the creeps. She was careful not to touch it as she made her way down. When she hit the bottom, she stood staring up and down an enormous tunnel made of ancient bricks covered with more of the green stuff. A thick sludge moved slowly along in the concrete ditch in the middle of the tunnel. The smell was indescribable.

With her purple T-shirt pulled over her nose, she walked along a ledge beside the river of smell. The air was damp and a growing fear of being lost forever was growing inside her chest. Tears leaked out of her eyes unnoticed. Why had she come down here? She was usually so sane and this was definitely the act of an unbalanced person.

She followed the narrow beam of her light until she came to a metal ladder leading up. Should she climb it? When she shined the beam to the top of the ladder, she spotted another one of those circular openings. She had no idea where it would take her so she slogged along.

The sewer narrowed and the ledge she walked along got skinnier. When she rounded a corner, it disappeared altogether and the sludge ran between the bars of a metal grid that completely blocked her passage. She longed to sit down and think, but sitting was not an option. A sob tore from her throat and she wiped the tears off her face. She was lost in the underground. What could be worse than this?

"Hey, you don't belong down here."

The voice startled her and she almost fell into the ditch of stink. She took her shirt off her nose and gagged. The smell was so thick she was afraid to breath. "I'm lost," she squeaked.

A figure loomed out of the darkness. It was a boy about the same age as Logan. He carried a hover board in a pack on his back, had long blond hair in dreadlocks, and very white skin. The boy laughed. "I guessed that. Why'd you come down here?"

Shayna straightened and smoothed her hair. "I'm looking for someone."

"Down here? Who?"

"His name is Logan. I met him yesterday at the hospital. He said he lives down here. I thought finding him would be easy."

The boy took several long strides and towered over her. "You're looking for Logan? I find that pretty hard to believe. You're from topside. Citizens from topside don't come into the sewers. Citizens from topside are messed up on Sopore." He shined the beam of a huge Maglite in her face. "You don't look stoned at all."

She clutched her purse to her chest and pulled her jacket close. "I'm allergic to corn," she whispered. "Do you know Logan?"

The boy backed up a step. "Him and I are buds. We make runs together."

"Can you take me to him?"

"He's topside right now scooping some Intel so he can save a friend."

"Raj," she said. "I saw the Enforcers take him."

"You did? Logan told me he was gonna get Raj out or die tryin'. He feels responsible. Stupid, nobody can be responsible for someone else's luck. Raj had the bad luck and now he's payin'."

Hot fear for Logan poured through Shayna's veins. "He can't do that. No one can. Once the Company has you, you're done. They watch everything. They watch everyone. They know everything. They're probably listening to us right now."

The boy shined his huge beam on the brick roof, panning it up and down the tunnel. Three rats ran along a narrow ledge high above. Shayna squeaked. "Rats."

"They won't bother you and there ain't no Ears in this tunnel. Too much moisture ruins electronics. No Sniffers either. We're pretty safe. At least I am. You're lost."

Shayna took a deep breath and instantly regretted it. "How can you stand the stench?"

The boy shrugged. "You can get used to lots of things . . . if you have to. What's your name, girl?"

"Shhh . . . Shayna."

He stuck out a hand much like Logan's, rough and covered with leather gloves with the fingers cut out. "I'm Enoch, better known as Knock. Come on, I'll take you to Dr. Goswami. Maybe he can figure out what to do with you."

"As in knock knock?"

"Yeah, you got a problem with that?"

"No, if that's what people call you I'm fine with it. And no one has to do anything with me. I came down here to see Logan. If he's not here, then please escort me back to the surface."

"He'll be back 'fore long. I told you already, he's on a mission topside. I just got back from up there and I ain't in the mood to return. If you can't find your own way, then you'll just have to go with me."

Shayna sighed. *What a contradictory individual.* "Lead the way then, uh, Knock. I guess I have no choice but to go with you."

He laughed as he turned and walked the ledge heading in the direction she'd come. "You got that right, girly."

Logan rotated slowly, hunting for SS. He spotted a woman dressed in a black rain coat wearing sunglasses and shrunk against the bridge support. She had to be SS. He watched her for a minute. When she ambled toward the playground, he turned and stared at the tan bricks of the support.

Taking a deep breath, he keyed the memory app. The air shimmered and a dumpster popped into view. As he was thinking *what the heck?* he saw a doughy hand reach into the trash and pull out a crumpled bag filled with doughnuts. This had to be a Hump memory. The air abruptly shimmered again and he actually felt his dad's arm around his waist. He closed his eyes for a moment and when he opened them he saw letters across the top of each lens of the glasses, "Keep your eyes open."

Logan forced his eyes to remain open as shivers of fear and sadness washed through him. He shrugged the debilitating feelings off and concentrated as he rose through a shimmering haze. He could smell the soap his dad always used to shave. He could feel the strength of his dad's chest behind him and the strong comforting arm around his body. Tears ran out of his eyes. He missed his father so much. He wanted to turn and look at his dad. He wanted to see his father's face one more time, but the hole in the wall appeared and he had to concentrate.

He saw the hole and looked inside. The memory app created a tunnel around his body. He had to focus really hard to hold onto his vision. Most of the memories were sensory. He heard his dad breathing and the sound of cars traveling across the bridge overhead. He smelled the damp air of a New York summer night close to the East River and his father's familiar scent. Seeing things was harder. The things he saw were encased in a tunnel that shimmered around the edges. It was so weird.

He spotted the burlap sack deep in the recess. He heard his father laugh from far away as though through water, and then he was put back on the ground. "That's for emergencies, Logan," his dad said. "One day you're gonna need it. Remember where it is, because if anything should happen to me, this is for you."

His Dad took a brick and scratched an L in the surface with the blade of his pocket knife, then slathered mortar on it.

The memories were so poignant Logan's heart felt as though it would break. He held back floods of tears as his father's large, callused hand shoved the brick into place, the L clearly visible. When Logan had the brick's position firmly in his mind, he clicked the memory app off. He couldn't take it anymore.

The air shimmered again and Logan bent over to take several deep breaths. He was never going to see his father again. He needed to move on. The emotions were making him weak. He couldn't afford the luxury of sadness or love.

Squaring his shoulders, he stood up and immediately spotted the brick with the L. It had faded over time but the first letter of his name was still there.

The brick looked like all the others, the mortar worn and dirty. He took his pack off and removed a small chisel he'd taken from Eddie's lab. He checked again to make sure the woman was gone. Two agents walked slowly toward the city on the bridge. It looked like he had a few minutes.

He used the chisel to chip away the mortar. At one point, he almost quit. This was stupid. He'd been six, his father had had five more years to retrieve his treasure, years Logan was growing up and learning to live underground. Once his dad had gone underground to live, Logan rarely walked topside and most of the time he had no idea where his dad went. They were hungry and poor. Surely his dad would have retrieved the treasure so they could live.

When Logan had most of the mortar around the edges of the brick removed, he saw there was more under the brick but none over it. While using the memory app, he'd seen his dad insert the brick with mortar on the bottom only.

Filled with renewed hope, Logan loosened the brick with the chisel and pulled. It slid out slowly. Some of the bricks around chipped off and the brick made a loud scraping noise. He glanced around for the hundredth time, but no one was in the park at all. Even the woman pushing the baby was gone.

The brick fell into his hand and he flicked on the light icon on Hump's glasses by saying, "light on." A pencil-thin beam illuminated the interior of the hole. The space was there. For a minute, Logan thought it was empty. His stomach lurched when he spotted the faint bump of a dust-covered bag deep in the hole.

Logan held his breath as he reached into the deep recess. The burlap sack was heavy and filled with several lumpy objects. He had to manipulate it to get it out of the hole. Twice he glanced over his shoulder looking for the woman agent. He spotted her walking slowly around the kiddy playground with one finger on her glasses. She could head back this way at any second.

When he had the bag in his hand, he ran for the shadows between the supports and hunkered down next to the huge structure with the bridge high above. He felt safe for the moment, safe enough to open the bag and see what treasure his father had left to him.

The first thing he pulled out was a strange garment. It shimmered with iridescent hues of green, red and blue. There was a note taped to it in his father's handwriting. It said, "Put this on."

He pulled off his dirty, blue hooded sweatshirt and turned the strange garment over in his hands. The fabric looked more like fish scales than cloth but it felt slithery smooth. It was almost like rubber. He found the opening and shrugged into it. The minute it was on, it adhered to him like skin. The long sleeves were tight and covered half his hand. There was a hood. He pulled it over his hair and it closed around his head. When it was on, it felt like a wet suit, tight, but flexible. He stared at his arm and gasped. His arm was almost invisible against the bricks of the bridge support. The color of the material had changed to tan and completely blended into the bricks. This cloth reacted like a chameleon's skin, changing color to match the background. When he dropped his arm to the grass, it shimmered for a second and turned green. Wow! What a cool gift, but it couldn't be the treasure.

He reached deeper into the bag and pulled out a small gold bar. It was heavy, maybe as much as ten pounds. With gold selling for over five thousand an ounce, this one bar could be worth more than eighty thousand credits. He found two more bars and sat back on his heels. This should be enough to buy his way to the moon.

There was one more lump in the bag. He reached in and found a silver disk. It was almost half an inch thick and three inches in diameter. He turned it over and over examining all angles. He saw a spot for a thumb print and touched it. His father must have keyed it to him. The air shivered and a four-level structure opened in three-D. It was a hologram. He could see into the structure from all angles. A bad feeling slammed into his gut and he glanced over his shoulder. The woman was racing toward him with a stunner in her hands.

Chapter Seven

Logan ran from the female agent, dodging between trees and through clumps of shrubbery. He had to get back across the river. With the bridge compromised, his only option was the Broadway tunnel where the number-two and three subway lines ran under the river.

When he glanced over his shoulder, he didn't see anyone. Maybe he'd lost her. He ran for the closest station on Clark Street. Clark was two blocks away when he turned and saw the female agent had been joined by two men. Then he remembered his new jacket. It was his only chance. If the chameleon suit didn't work, he was going to the moon as a prisoner and all his father's gifts would be taken away from him.

He dodged between two buildings and spotted a massive trash Dumpster behind a restaurant. He had only a few seconds before the SS turned into the alley. He dived into the garbage, digging deep through the trash and pulling it over his lower body and his face. He had a piece of brown paper that had probably contained fish over his face and clumps of food refuse which included rotting lettuce, beet pulp and spoiled pasta over his legs. He lay still, breathing shallowly through his mouth. The stench was too strong to draw in through his nose. He'd end up gagging.

The sound of running feet approached and he stopped breathing altogether. Voices talking into their com glasses filtered down to him. "Lost him. He's got to be here. Check the Dumpster."

Logan heard footsteps next to his head. The trash was stirred and lifted with a stick. He lay frozen in place. Would the chameleon suit work?

The stick lifted a piece of trash off his body and prodded deeply right next to him. This was it. They were going to find him. Then he heard. "Nothing in here but smell. Damn this thing reeks."

"He has to be here," the female agent's voice rose to an irritated whine.

"I'm sorry, Mrs. Weiner, there's no one here. He must have found a hole underground and bolted."

"Then we need to check the Broadway Tunnel. He'll have to get across the river some way." Her nasal voice resounded with authority. She was in charge.

"Yes, ma'am."

Logan heard them running back down the alley, but he didn't move. He knew it could be a ploy to draw him out. He started counting slowly as he listened. When he reached three thousand, he figured it had almost been an hour. He'd take a peek.

He pulled the chameleon hood low and as quietly as he could rose onto his knees and looked up and down the alley. It appeared to be empty. If the agents were in the Number Two, he was going back over the bridge. He still had a chip and a credit disk. He'd take the bus back to Harlem and the straightest shot home.

The sun had set. The bridge was lighted with sodium vapor lights casting a yellow glow over the concrete and the river. It started to drizzle. Logan pulled the hood up and walked fast. When he looked up, he could see the rain falling in sheets through yellow light.

A sigh of relief whooshed out of his lungs when he reached the other side. He jogged for the bus stop on Allen and Second Avenue. The stop was empty. The entire city was empty. People on Sopore retired early.

He stepped into an alcove where he hoped there were no cameras and waited for the bus. When it came, he leaped on board and sighed. No doubt he was on camera crossing the bridge and getting on the bus, but maybe because they thought he would go underground no one would notice him getting on the bus. They didn't know he had a chip and a credit disk. They didn't know he could stay top side, but that wouldn't matter if some topsider manning a watch station caught a glimpse of him getting on the bus and reported it.

When he got to Harlem, he got off the bus and looked in all directions. The city streets were empty. The rain created huge puddles that reflected neon signs flashing on closed stores and huge Company billboards. "Get a new life. Sign up to build a colony in space. Freedom is only a few light years away. Sign up NOW!"

Signs like that were all over the cities. The Company was ramping up its mining operations and opening new planets all the time for colonies and mining companies. They needed warm bodies, any warm body.

Logan ran through the downpour to Eddie's shop. Eddie ran a Radio Shack with the least business of any store on earth. The door was always unlocked. He ducked inside and a bell rang somewhere deep under the shop. The shelves were filled with electronic gadgets from the twenty-first century when the store had opened. Tablets and laptop computers sat on shelves covered with dust beside ancient I-Phones and other com units Logan did not recognize.

He knew the way down. He hit the cash button on the old register. The drawer flew open . . . it was empty, and a door appeared behind him. Laughing at the absurdity of the shop, he climbed into a tube leading down. Using the rungs of an old rusty ladder, he quickly descended into the real business.

Eddie and Hump were there to greet him. "You made it?" Eddie said but it was more of a question.

"Nice duds, man." Eddie fingered his chameleon suit. "Where'd you get this?"

"It was with my father's things."

"This is super high-tech military issue," Eddie said. "It's made from organic material found on a moon orbiting PH2b. I heard it's even blaster and stunner proof."

Logan smiled. "Look what it does." He put his arm next to Eddie's purple shirt. The sleeve rapidly changed to an exact match.

"Whoa!" Hump said. "That's like so rad."

Eddie snagged Logan's pack. "What else did you find?"

Logan grabbed a strap. Did he really trust Eddie? Did he trust anyone? "Swear you won't try to jack me."

Eddie dropped the strap. His slanted eyes narrowed. "You think I'd do that to you?"

Logan shrugged. "Guess not. I'm pretty paranoid. This is Raj's life . . . and all I have left of my father."

Logan glanced at the memory app and his world shimmered. When he looked down he was wearing a black suit coat, a white shirt and he could see the end of a black tie. *What?* Then it was gone and Logan shuddered. Something was definitely not right.

Eddie stood in front of him grinning and holding out his hand. "You okay, Loge?"

Logan shook off the disturbing image. Had it been his memory or someone else's close by . . . like Eddie's or Hump's. "My father left this to me, you know, and he's gone."

"I respect that, dude," Eddie said. "Family is everything. Remember, I loaned you a chip and credit. We're in this together."

Logan opened the bag and took out one of the bars of gold. "Is this enough to get me to the moon?"

Eddie gripped the bar and hefted it in two hands. "Heavy, maybe ten pounds. The price of gold is skyrocketing. This bar should buy passage on one of the Tong's ships no problem. You got more?"

Logan's sense of unease would not go away. When he glanced at Eddie's friend Hump, he saw naked avarice gleaming from pale blue eyes. Logan took the gold bar back and placed it inside the bag. He reached into his pack and removed the stunner. Eddie's eyebrows shot up and Logan shrugged. "I know you, but him, I never met before. How do I know he's cool?"

Logan laid the stunner across his lap. He had his knife in a sheath on his belt, but he still felt uneasy. He glanced from Hump to Eddie and sighed. He needed Eddie's help or this would never get off the ground. Eddie had the Tong contacts and the tech backup. Logan pulled the silver disk out of his father's bag and showed it to Eddie. "Ever seen anything like this before?"

Logan thumbed it and the three-D hologram appeared. Eddie sucked in a huge breath. "Holy crap!"

"Do you recognize it? Where is this building? Dad thought it was important or he wouldn'ta put it in the bag."

Eddie walked all around the hologram, bending low, looking into all the rooms and levels. "This, my friend, is a three-D blueprint of the Palin Lunar Penitentiary. How did your dad get this?"

Logan gasped. "The moon prison?"

Eddie nodded. "Oh yeah."

"My dad worked for Titan Construction. Didn't they build the prison? I think they planned to send him there."

Eddie bent over again and looked at the lower levels. "There might be a back door into this thing."

Hump shoved Logan aside and stuck out his hand. "I'll take that and the bag."

Logan and Eddie backed up together. "What the . . .?" Eddie snarled.

Hump's entire demeanor had changed. He stood straighter, appeared ten pounds lighter and he was pointing a very frightening military-issue blaster at them. He grabbed Logan's com glasses, put them on, tapped the ear piece and spoke into it. "Agent six-nine-seven reporting. Two Vagrants in custody."

For the one second Hump took to tap on the glasses and speak, Logan knew from experience, his eyes would be focused on the screen displayed in the glasses. The memory app was still active which could add another second of confusion. This was his only chance. He tackled Eddie and knocked him to the floor. Hump fired the blaster. Logan felt heat rush into his chest, but he didn't burst into flames. He ignored the pain, flipped over and fired the stunner at Hump on full strength.

Hump froze, fell to the floor and began seizing. His feet drummed on the puke-green linoleum, and the smell of urine filled the air. Logan leaped to his feet. "We gotta get him out of here. They'll track his signal and find your lab."

Eddie pulled himself to his feet using a desk. "I can't believe it. I've known him for almost a year." Eddie wiped his brow and pushed limp black hair off his forehead. He touched the black mark on Logan's chameleon suit that was rapidly disappearing. "This suit saved your life."

Logan nodded. "We don't have much time. What do we do with him?"

"Sewers," Eddie snapped.

Between the two of them, they were able to drag Hump through the airlock and into the sewer below. "He can never go topside again," Logan said. "He knows too much. Maybe we should just kill him."

Eddie was bent over, sucking in huge breaths. Hump was no lightweight. "Could you really do that? Kill a man?"

Logan thought about it. In the heat of the moment maybe, but in cold blood like this, just waste a guy . . . "Not like this."

"You'll have to take him to the mole people and let them deal with him."

Logan groaned. Dragging this fat asshole through the underground was going to be a disgusting, back-breaking chore. "Find me some rope."

Chapter Eight

By the time Logan had Hump safely underground he was exhausted and it was close to midnight. Running the tunnels alone was one thing, running them while dragging two-hundred pounds of human trussed like a soy-protein roast, was a whole different deal. He'd had to take easier paths and a more round-about route. Twice he'd picked up a Sniffer and then lost it in wet tunnels. Hump was now nicely coated with sewage and slime.

He pushed through the door to the Professor's lab and received the shock of his life. Shayna was sitting calmly at his desk drinking tea. The Professor stood up abruptly. "Logan, my good boy, what have you brought to me?"

"Nothing you want," Logan said as he released the rope he'd wrapped around his waist and over one shoulder. He slicked back his sweaty hair and smiled shyly. "Shayna, why are you here?"

The Professor walked around him and nudged Hump with one black-booted foot. "Who is he?"

"This is a Company agent. He tried to arrest me and Eddie and take my inheritance. I have no idea what his real name is. He calls himself Hump."

The Professor picked up a whistle he wore on a cord around his neck and blew three sharp blasts. Two mole people rushed into the room. When they came in, Shayna moved behind Logan. "Who are they?"

"The Prof has his own Enforcers. Vandy and Sly, meet Shayna. She's a topsider."

The two mole people wore a crazy mish mash of clothing. Vandy's camo pants, tie-dyed pink shirt and ratty torn, tan, hooded jacket contrasted wildly with Sly's green tartan kilt, blue-felt leggings, thick mohair sweater, original color unknown, and dreadlocks tucked in a knit cap. Sly's skin was the color of coffee with no cream and Vandy's skin was the color of the cream with no coffee. They were both over six-feet tall, thin and loose-limbed.

They bowed stiffly. "Nice to meet you, ma'am," Vandy said.

"Bet you never saw anything like them topside."

Shayna's laugh was a nervous giggle. "No, nothing like them."

"Take him to the brig." The Professor's eyes were locked with Vandy's and he was pointing at Hump. "We'll soften him up and talk to him later. A few days with no Sopore and he should be willing to tell us anything he knows in exchange for a swallow of soda."

Logan put his hand in the small of Shayna's back and urged her toward the door. "How did you find the Professor? Have you seen any of my world yet?"

"I wanted to see you again," Shayna said with her head turned away from him. A rosy flush was slowly rising in her cheeks. "I got lost in one of the subway tunnels and your friend Enoch found me. He brought me to Professor Goswami." She looked over her shoulder as they stepped through the door. "He's so nice. Like a real . . ."

"You were gonna say person, weren't you?"

"Logan, I'm so sorry, I know you're real people. I just never imagined anything like this place. Everyone says the mole people are mutants and monsters and the Vagrants will kill you for your chip and your credit disk."

Logan took her hand. "Well, now that you've seen mole people and Vagrants, it's time to see how we live."

Her hand felt warm and alive in his and his heart sang with the excitement of being with her again. She'd come looking for him, down here, in the worst place on the planet. She must really like him.

He led her down the long tunnel leading from the Professor's lab to one of the central tunnels of the underground. He turned left and they walked hand in hand down the softly-lighted path.

"What makes the blue light?" She asked.

"We grow a special phosphorescent fungus to light our city. We're never in the dark."

They exited the tunnel into a huge vaulted cavern. Shayna stopped and looked up. "This is amazing. I never knew there were caves like this under the city."

"There are old tunnels down here excavated in the early nineteenth century." Logan pointed at the floor. "Right under us is a network dug in 1896."

The cavern was filled with shops. Most were closed for the night. Three huge chandeliers dangled from the ceiling lighting everything with the brilliance of two-hundred watt bulbs. Neon signs blinked above the small stores and kiosks advertising fresh vegetables, medicine, electronics, clothing, pets and more. "You can buy anything you want down here," Logan said. "But credit disks don't work."

Shayna's dark eyes flew open. "Then how would you pay?"

Logan led her down one narrow alley into a well-lit side tunnel. "We barter," he said. "Everyone down here either makes something they can sell or works in one of the grow-light farms and receives vegetables or soy protein as wages. Runners go topside and buy or steal things to trade for Sopore-free food. No one down here wants to be an addict. Everyone down here works at something."

"And what do you do?"

He grinned. "You know what I do. I'm a runner for the Professor."

He took her down a narrower cavern lined with small tables and chairs and little stands. The sound of Frank Sinatra singing *Are You Lonesome Tonight* drifted through the air. Shayna squeezed his hand. "Someone down here likes Sinatra?"

"Large Marge does and she runs a little tea shop that's always open. Can I buy you a cup of tea?"

Shayna grinned. "Of course you can. I'd love that."

Halfway down the row of closed restaurants and tea shops was a small stand with a blinking Open sign. Logan pulled a chair out for Shayna and she sat down. "And where's Large Marge?"

"She likes to play mahjong. She'll be in the back with her friends. I'll get her."

Logan pushed behind the stand and found Marge in the back hunched over a folding table with three other women. Marge was a big woman, at least three hundred pounds. Her friends looked up. They were all oriental, probably an eclectic blend of Chinese, Korean, Vietnamese and Japanese. Marge was all Chinese. Her real name was Margaret Woo but everyone knew her as Marge.

When Marge looked up and saw Logan, a huge grin split her face and she lurched to her feet. She walked hunched over, supporting herself by leaning on a side table, a dresser and then the counter. Her feet were always swollen, her back hurt, she was diabetic and had high blood pressure. When she got close enough, she grabbed Logan and hugged him, then spouted off a long string of Chinese to her friends. They jabbered back. Logan understood maybe half of it and it made him blush.

"What for you in my shop this late, boy?" Marge asked with her meaty arm still wrapped around his shoulders.

"I have a friend and uh . . . we came by for tea and one of your almond cookies."

Marge squeezed his shoulders. "A female friend?"

Logan could only nod. All Marge's friends shrieked with laughter.

Marge leaned in close. She smelled of strange spices, tea, oranges and cedar. "I make you love tea?"

"No, no, just some Oolong Superior with honey, if you have it." Logan paused. "And cookies?"

Marge laughed. "You know I always have honey. My hives are in Master Zou's garden. He grows lots of squash and melons. They flower all the time."

Logan would owe Marge for the tea. It was rare and one of the few products Monsonta was unable to adulterate with Sopore. He pushed through the curtain separating the back of Marge's tea stall from the front and returned to Shayna. Frank was singing *Love is a Many Splendored Thing* as he took a seat opposite Shayna. He wanted to take her hand. He'd imagined this moment and now it was actually happening. She looked incredibly lovely and for a second he couldn't speak.

"Was she back there? I heard laughing." Shayna said.

Logan nodded. "She lives back there. We're getting her best tea and cookies."

"She must really like you."

Logan nodded. "After my dad was picked up and shipped off world, she kind of looked after me. Her and the Professor."

"Your dad was a criminal?"

Marge chose that moment to waddle out from behind the stand with a small lacquer-wood tray in her hand. A porcelain tea pot and two small cups sat on the tray next to a bottle of honey and a plate of cookies. She towered over them, holding onto the counter with one hand and the tray with the other.

"She very pretty," Marge said. "But she don't belong down here. She a topsider."

Marge placed the tray on the table and backed away. Her round face was filled with concern, her eyebrows were together and her bow mouth tight.

"She came down here by herself to see me, Marge. That says everything."

Marge smiled, but shook her head. "She pretty, probably *hapa haoli*, part white, part Japanese, but no good gonna come of this, boy child, no good."

She turned and shuffled back behind the curtain. A spate of Chinese wafted out of the room behind the stall.

"Pay no attention to her," Logan said. "She thinks she's my mother and she hates topsiders. Most people down here have a pretty crappy opinion of them."

Logan poured steaming, fragrant tea into the two small cups and offered Shayna the honey jar. "No corn in anything," he said. "We know better."

"I feel pretty weird now," she said. "She looked at me like I was a cockroach."

"Now you know how I feel when I go topside."

Shayna stirred her tea, held it to her nose and sniffed. "This smells like heaven." She sipped. "I never thought of it like that. I never thought about the people down here as real people with lives and stuff. Wow, this tea is really good."

"Have a cookie," Logan said. "Yeah, we're real, we have families and lives just like you topsiders. We struggle to live. We have criminals and drug addicts and bad people, but we're real, we're not trapped by the government in some awful drug-induced fog. And nobody watches us. No cameras underground unless the Company put them down here."

Shayna nodded. "I feel like I'm seeing my life and what living up there means for the first time. Am I like, the only topsider who ever came down here and realized this?"

"No, you'd be surprised at how many of us Vagrants came down here voluntarily. I mean most had no choice. They lost their jobs like my dad, or they did something wrong and got caught doing it on some Company camera." He finally got the nerve to reach out and touch her hand. "You and me, we're an odd pair aren't we? Gonna tell me why you came looking for me?"

Shayna's squirmed under his searching look but allowed him to hold her hand. "I don't really know." She took her hand away so she could hold her cup. "You're so different from anyone I've ever met." She sipped the tea. "This is yummy."

"Is that it? I'm different?"

She put her cup down and cradled it between two hands. "I guess I felt like we made some kind of connection that day at the hospital. You and your friend were so alive. Everyone up there is dead." She waved her hand to indicate his underground world. "This feels like real life. Up there . . . it's like we're all in a bad, boring movie that never ends. It's clean to the point of being sterile. When your friend got taken away, I felt like I saw my world for the first time. It's wrong. The people up there that run everything, they're bad. They control everyone and everything and move people around like pieces on a chess board. I went home and suddenly I couldn't be there anymore." She shook her head and stared at the steaming cup. "I want to be alive, too. I want to help save your friend."

They sat there drinking their tea for several moments. Logan pushed the plate of cookies toward her. "Try one."

Shayna took a cookie and nibbled. "Good," she mumbled. "You're going to try to save him aren't you? Your friend?"

Logan nodded. "I am. They already lifted him to the moon. I'm going after him."

"How can you do that? The moon . . . it's a giant space station and prison controlled by the Company. And the Lift." She shuddered. "I don't even like the elevators in my building. The Lift goes like four thousand miles an hour."

"I think it goes faster than that." Logan sipped his tea, enjoying the sweetness of the honey and the fragrant flavor of the tea. "I haven't quite figured out how I'm gonna save Raj, but I'm workin' on it."

Chapter Nine

Logan took Shayna back to the Professor's lab. Even though he enjoyed her company and kind of liked her, he felt it would be better if she went home. Marge was right. She didn't belong down here.

"I don't want to go home," Shayna insisted as they went through the door leading to the Professor's lab. "I want to help you rescue Raj."

"Well you can't. What about your parents? They'll call the authorities and start looking for you. You can't stay here. You'll start some kind of crazy hunt and it'll end up involving us and get people down here in trouble. I'm gonna buy passage to the moon on a Tong ship. You can't go with me. Rescuing Raj is about an impossible mission, but I have to try. Raj was just a kid. He doesn't deserve to get sent off to some mining planet like my dad. You're not involved and you really shouldn't be." He stopped and stared down at her. "Why do you want to help anyway?"

When she shrugged, her long black hair rippled like silk across her shoulders. She wore a simple white blouse under a black silk jacket that reached her knees, a black skirt and real leather boots that came to only an inch or two from the silk jacket's hemline. She was the prettiest girl Logan had ever seen and the more he was with her the more he liked her, but she needed to go home or she was going to distract him from the job at hand which was rescuing Raj.

"I feel like my life has no meaning," she said. "Up there, you go to school because you have to and then they assign you a job. You don't get to choose, you just do what the Company says for the rest of your life. I guess that's okay if you're a freaking zombie like my mom and dad, but I'm not doped to the gills. I want a real life. I want to do something that has meaning, like saving Raj. Let me help."

Logan threw up his hands. "We'll talk to the Professor and see what he says. If you won't go back, he's gonna have to find you a place to stay. But you can't go with me to the moon. Maybe the Professor can find something for you to do." He groaned and muttered. "I don't have time for this."

She took his hand. "I won't get in the way. I promise. Let me stay with you?"

Frustration was making Logan crazy. Part of him wanted her to stay, but now was the wrong time. Why did Raj have to get taken? If that one event hadn't happened, he could stay here with Shayna. Maybe she could even be his girlfriend; but Raj had to be saved. It was the only thing on his mind. He was focused on it and the rescue was going to go down.

The Professor wasn't in the lab. Logan figured he was softening Hump up, which was not something Shayna should see. He led her through the lab into the second subway car of the Professor's home, past the rows of fragrant herbs and medicinal plants growing in hydroponic solution under banks of Gro-lights, through the second hydro car and into the two cars that made up their living quarters. "You can stay here for the night," he told Shayna. "I have to find the Professor."

She sat on the lumpy couch that might have been green at one time . . . or maybe blue. "Will you come back?"

He nodded. "I have a room back there." He pointed toward a door at the rear of the car that went into the last car in the tunnel. Beyond their sleeping car was a tunnel carved out of the living rock in the nineteenth century.

He handed Shayna a small hand-held device. "You can play games on this and if I need to call you, it's a com unit, too. The bathroom is over there and the kitchen. The Professor might have food in the fridge or the cabinets. He usually has something to eat."

She took his hand. He was standing over her. Their eyes met. "Can I wait in your room?"

Holy crap! "Why?"

"I'll feel safer there."

Logan stifled a groan. Could this get any worse? "I guess." He paused, his heart leaping around in his chest like a jack rabbit. "If you really want to."

She got off the couch and he led her through the door and into a short hallway down the center of the car. "The Professor's room is that one. I sleep here."

He pushed a curtain aside and led her into his small cubicle. The walls were lined with bookshelves filled with all kinds of old books; paperbacks, classics, a huge atlas, books of maps of the world, history books in several languages, and text books. His bed was more of a cot pushed against a wall under more shelves. All but one of the old subway car's windows had been painted black. That one window looked out on a rock wall with water dribbling down the sharp stones to a pond sitting in a small declivity.

"My waterfall," Logan said. The tinkle of the water could be clearly heard.

"It's a very peaceful sound," she said. "You like to read? Why don't you use a reader?"

Logan nodded. "I do, but I like the feel of a real book. There's something magic about the written word. I can read in four different languages. Marge taught me Chinese and I read Spanish,

French and Japanese. I don't understand the spoken language as well as the written. Marge talks way too fast."

Shayna sat down on his bed. "I'll wait here. It's nice. I like your room."

Logan shrugged. He wanted to run. Her being here was great, but so sudden. He couldn't wrap his head around it. He needed time. He'd never had a girlfriend and wasn't sure he was ready for one now. Life underground was full of risk. "I'll keep you posted on the com link and I'll sleep on the couch."

She nodded and smiled. "I'll be fine here. It feels safe."

Logan rolled his eyes. "No place on Earth is safe, especially no place underground. I'll check in with you later."

Logan jogged all the way to the brig. He figured that's where the Professor would be and he needed to get some distance between him and Shayna to think. What was he going to do with her?

He found the Professor and Enoch standing over Hump who was tied to a metal table with thick leather straps. The big agent was shivering and his pale skin had taken on a gray hue.

"He jonesin' already?"

"Not really." The Professor held up a huge glass syringe with a large gauge needle attached to it. It was half-filled with yellow fluid. "I gave him something to hurry the process along."

Logan nodded. The Vagrants had developed a flush to remove the Sopore. Sometimes a runner would get accidentally poisoned by the drug or they'd get an escapee that needed cleansing.

Hump began a low wail and started shaking harder.

"He might start seizing shortly," the Professor said. "Then we can get down to business."

Knock moved from his position on the other side of the table to stand next to Logan. "What did you do with the chick?"

The Professor glanced at them and lifted one eyebrow. Logan could feel his face heating with embarrassment. "She's uh, she's in my room." *Oh god why did he have to say that?*

Knock guffawed and the Professor choked. "In your room?" The Professor said. "What were you thinking?"

"She wanted to stay there." Logan turned away so they wouldn't see his acute embarrassment. This was way worse than he thought it would be. "I tried to make her go, I swear."

"You're allowing her to stay underground?" the Professor said. "Do you think that is a wise idea?"

"Of course it's not a wise idea," Logan snapped. He held up his hands, palms flat and grimaced. "I wanted her to go home. I told her to go. I don't have time for this right now." He blew out an enormous sigh. "What was I supposed to do? She wouldn't leave."

The Professor shook his head. "We will have to proceed as though she is not here. What do you have in the rucksack?" He pointed to the pack Logan had brought with him.

Logan grinned. "I found my father's stash. He left me some cool stuff." Logan pointed to his chest. "I found this awesome suit. Look it changes color like a chameleon." He put his arm against Knock's maroon hoody and the chameleon fabric obliged him by turning a deep burgundy shade to match.

The Professor touched it. "This is a very rare material found only on one planet. I believe it is the skin of a lizard-like creature. It should also repel bullets. What else did he leave you?"

Logan pulled the disk out and thumbed it. "This and some gold. I have enough to buy passage on a Tong ship to their moon base."

The three-D image of the Palin Penitentiary opened up. The Professor gasped and backed up. "That is a very valuable and very illegal set of blueprints." He bent over and looked under it. He traced several passages among the four levels with one finger. "I believe this could be a back door, probably for bringing in materials for the construction." He stood up and rubbed his back in an abstract manner. "If they didn't close it up after construction, it could be a way to get inside." He shook his head. "I can't see why they would close it. Who can get to the moon if they don't ride the Lift and that's controlled by the Company? And it's not like there's a lot of foot traffic." He grinned. "But if you find this doorway and get inside, what do you do once you're in there?"

"Eddie is doing some research, trying to find out where they keep the younger conscripts. They have to separate them, don't they? I mean Raj is just a kid."

The Professor moved to the other side of the hologram and pointed. "These are cells for violent criminals and murderers." He pointed to another section. "The symbol on this area says it's a holding area for transportees. There are several large rooms and sanitation facilities over here. This should be where Raj is being held." The Professor rocked back on his heels. "This is a suicide mission, Loge. You're gonna die doing this."

"Then I'll die," Logan said. "Life underground is pretty cheap, you know. How many of us make it to old age? How many of us runners make it ten years without getting caught and transported? If I'm gonna die young anyway, I might as well go out trying to do something impossible, something that's never been done." He grinned. "I'll be a legend."

VAGRANT

The Professor's old eyes glistened with unshed tears. "I understand. I know who you are, I knew your father. You're a hero. It's in your blood. You don't have to prove yourself."

A long loud groan from the man on the table got their attention. "Please . . ." Hump moaned. "I'm dying."

The Professor leaned over Hump, lifted his eyelids and shined a penlight into each eye. "You're not dying. You're just doing without your drug for the first time in your life, I imagine."

Hump arched his back, screamed and drummed his heels on the table. White spittle flew from his thick lips. "Then give me some. Oh, God, it hurts."

The Professor leaned in close again. "This is what your Company feeds its people. You did this to yourself." He took a can of a popular energy drink and held it where Hump could see. "This can of Demon Venom holds enough Sopore to put a small Vagrant child into a coma. Corn syrup," he pointed to the label on the back. "It's in everything."

"Please, let me have just a small sip."

"You must answer some questions first."

Hump turned his head away. "I can't. They'll kill me."

The Professor took the can and slowly poured its contents onto Hump's chest. The brown liquid splashed and a drop fell on Hump's chin. He struggled to get his tongue on it.

"If you don't tell us, we'll prolong your withdrawal for a very long time. In fact, we can prolong it indefinitely if we so choose."

Hump wailed. "What do you want from me?"

The Professor glanced at Logan and winked. "Now we're talking."

.

Chapter Ten

Hump finally coughed up a slew of passwords for important data access, names of every agent he'd ever known, and by putting Eddie's glasses on Hump and using the Memory App, they were able to pull up the faces of those agents. Some of them shocked Logan who had seen many of them walking around in the subway. The most important thing Hump provided was the whereabouts of a key like the one Logan wore around his neck, a key that would open any fifth-level door.

Level five was the highest security level Hump had access to. There were only two levels higher and only senior Company officials and the CEO had those keys. Palin Penitentiary was a fifth-level facility. Logan couldn't believe his luck. If he could get Hump's key, he could walk into the moon prison like he owned it and open any door. The problem was going to be getting it.

The Professor sat across the narrow subway car he called home in an old seat nursing a cup of coffee ground from beans grown in the hydro car. Logan reclined on the couch and Shayna was sound asleep in Logan's room on the cot.

"Your friend, Hump, told us the door to his apartment is palm locked," the Professor said. "I am prepared to dig his chip out of his chunky hind end, but cutting off his hand is another thing altogether."

"Can we make a plasta-skin double of his palm print?"

The Professor sipped his coffee and sighed. "I have never tried such a thing. We could spray the compound onto his hand, allow it to harden and then use that as a mold. It might work, but the intricate patterns of a palm would be very hard to reproduce and the fingerprints would also have to be included. Getting it perfect would be difficult indeed."

Logan pulled the worn quilt covering his body under his chin. "I don't have a lot of time, Professor. I vote we just hack his hand off and I shove it into my pack. I use the chip to access the building and his hand to open the door. Simple, no fuss, won't take forever."

The Professor's grin showed shiny white teeth against his nut-brown skin. "You are a bloodthirsty child. I never imagined you'd grow up to be like this." He slurped his coffee and tilted his head. "The plasta-skin might work, but as you say, time is of the essence."

"Eddie already has a Tong vessel lined up for me. He paid them and they up ship in two days. I have to have that key."

The Professor rose and slapped his hands on his thighs. "Then tomorrow, Mr. Hump will be humanely put to sleep and his hand amputated. It will be up to the gods then." He tut-tutted. "Chopping off someone's arm for the purpose of stealing is such bad karma."

"It's for a good purpose," Logan said. "And I don't believe in karma or your gods for that matter. Hindu gods are freaking scarier than ten agents chasing you."

Logan shuddered and the Professor laughed. "To each his own. If you do not believe in my gods then what, young man, do you believe in?"

"I believe in myself." Logan pulled the covers over his head, rolled into the couch and passed out.

In the morning, Logan woke with a bubble of excitement lodged in his chest. He rolled over and saw Shayna and the

Professor creating something containing eggs and vegetables in the tiny kitchen. It smelled wonderful.

He sat up and Shayna brought him a cup of coffee. "This is so delicious," she said. "All we get above ground is Flavo-Caf and it's so full of corn syrup I could never drink it."

Logan took the cup and ran a hand over his wild hair. He needed to stop by Marge's and let her cut it. He usually kept it pretty short. "Thanks for the coffee," he said. He was almost afraid to look at her. She was so beautiful and he was just a tunnel rat.

Shayna laughed and Logan looked up surprised. He couldn't remember hearing her laugh. It was a happy carefree sound. Maybe she did like it down here.

"Professor Goswami and I just made breakfast. You don't know how great it is to be able to eat anything without examining all the ingredients. I have to be so careful up there. The doctors told my mom I could die if I ate any corn-derived product."

Logan blew across the top of his cup to cool the dark, fragrant liquid. "That's the one thing we don't have to worry about down here."

The Professor placed three plates on the tiny table pushed against blacked-out windows and they each sat down. Logan sat on a stool, the Professor his office chair and Shayna perched on the edge of an old subway seat. Logan ate his omelet slowly while watching Shayna between bites. He couldn't believe she was here eating with him like it was normal.

When they were done, she stood up and gathered their plates. "I'll wash up. The Professor said you have work to do."

Logan went into the sleeping car's tiny bathroom, took a shower and emerged feeling a lot fresher and wearing clean jeans and underclothes. He pulled his chameleon jacket over a skin-tight black T-shirt made from skin armor, a fabric designed to repel knife blades, and was ready for action. He had to get that key today.

The Professor was already in his special lab where Hump lay on the stainless-steel table with a black rubber mask over his face and his right arm extended on a smaller table. His arm and hand were coated with brown antiseptic all ready for the surgery. A quick pang of distaste and guilt washed through Logan. He squashed it. Hump was a spy and an agent for the Company. Who knew what dreadful deeds he'd done in their name. For sure, he'd been trying to catch Eddie and him and turn them in.

"If we keep it chilled, can you reattach it?" Logan asked.

"I can give you a dry-ice pack to put on it if you want, and when you get back I'll do my best."

Logan sighed. "It would make me feel better though why I have any sympathy for him is beyond me."

"You're a good and kind person, Logan. Between me, your father and Marge we instilled respect for human life into you along with a strong code of ethical behavior. This feels wrong to you because you are inflicting an injury on this man for something you perceive as selfish. You should not feel that way. What you do is for the good of someone else and possible many people. When you release Raj, save all the captured children you can."

"I will. I planned to all along."

Professor Goswami patted his arm. "I knew that."

The Professor's assistant came in wearing surgical scrubs and he left to prepare himself for the operation. Logan wasn't needed so he went hunting for Enoch. He found his friend eating at a small sushi stand in a section of the great cavern devoted to restaurants and food kiosks.

Logan pulled up a stool and leaned one elbow on the counter. "I have an important mission."

Knock stopped eating. "I know. You're going to the freaking moon."

"Not that. Hump has a level-five key. I have to get it."

Knock pushed the remains of two sushi rolls and sweet rice pudding away. "Level-five keys can go anywhere."

"Almost," Logan said.

"That and a chip can get you access to the freaking Lift. You could take it to the moon."

Logan shook his head. "Too many guards and agents know my face. I'd be caught in a minute. Hump's memory showed us a hundred agents. I recognized a lot of them from the subway. They're everywhere."

"Then what'd you need it for?"

"Palin Pen is a level-five facility. I can get in and out. I can open any locked door in the place."

"Uh, you do know there's no air on the moon." Knock pantomimed choking to death, holding one hand on his neck while he opened his mouth and gagged.

"No kidding. I'll have a suit."

"No gravity either."

"Jeez Knock, I know all this."

Knock turned and stared into his eyes. "Let me go with you and I'll help you snatch this key."

Logan couldn't meet his friend's gaze. He wanted Enoch with him. Going alone was frightening, but he couldn't ask his friend to put himself into such a dangerous position. "Why would you want to come? It's a suicide mission. I'm probably gonna die."

Knock laughed and shook his dreadlocks. "I know, dumbass, that's why I wanna go. What am I gonna do if you're gone? You're my best friend. Besides, this sounds like something I can really sink my teeth into. Stealing a level-five key would be awesome."

Logan slapped his friend on the back. "Dude, you're so radical."

"I know, always ready for your next crazy scheme." He looked thoughtful for a moment. "What you gonna do with the chick?"

"Who, Shayna?" Logan stared off in the general direction of his room. "Take her home, I guess."

Knock climbed off his stool and shook out his long black duster. The ragged hem brushed the tops of his old tennis shoes. "You got a lot to learn about women."

They walked slowly down the tunnel towards the Professor's place. "What do you mean by that?"

Knock grinned. "They *never* do what you think they should do. That's what."

They found Shayna cleaning the small cabinets in the Professor's kitchen. She had everything on the floor and was on her hands and knees scrubbing the insides. She scrambled to her feet when they walked in and shoved a stray strand of dark hair out of her eyes. When she saw both of them, she tilted her head and frowned. "What are you two planning?"

"I have something very important to do," Logan began.

She slapped her hands on her hips. "Don't tell me. I have to go home, right?"

Logan backed up a step. "It would be the best thing if you did. Your parents will miss you and call the Enforcers."

"I can't go back to that life, Logan. This is the first time I've ever felt so happy and alive. I don't ever want to go back. I don't care if my parents call the Enforcers. I'm just an object to them, their obligatory one child. Just thinking about that sterile, weird existence makes me want to scream. And besides, Professor Goswami said I could stay. He started some guys fixing up the little room at the end of the last car for me. You should see it. I already have a bed and shelves just like yours."

Logan groaned and glanced at Knock who was laughing. Knock threw up his hands. "Told you, dude. They never do what you want."

Chapter Eleven

Logan glanced over his shoulder. Shayna, dressed in black, skin-tight pants and black skin armor crawled along between him and Enoch who manned the rear. She'd insisted on coming along and the Professor had told them they might need her.

Hump's severed hand and a dry-ice pack were in a bag on Logan's back and he carried Eddie's chip in his pocket. Knock had Hump's chip in his pocket and Shayna, who as it turned out had a special chip designed to access all buildings in Harlem, didn't need to carry hers. It was still implanted in her hip.

The Professor thought it best they bring her because Hump's apartment was in Harlem. "She'll get you in and out a lot easier," he'd told Logan. "And her credit disk has no limit. You can ride the Loop if you need to or even grab a taxi."

Logan dropped out of the narrow, dark tunnel through a hole in the bottom and into the subway access. Shayna hung for a moment and dropped beside him followed by Knock. They pressed themselves flat against the wall afraid to make any noise. Above them an Ear blinked green. Logan pointed down the tunnel and they set off tiptoeing without making a sound.

When they reached a door in the rock wall, Logan used his third-level key to open it and they slid into a maintenance room filled with machinery and tools. Knock led the way through a hole in the roof which exited into a tunnel only three-feet high. They duck-walked down that passage until they reached the end where a steel ladder led up.

When they had gathered at the base of the ladder, Logan used the glasses to pull up a holographic map of the subway system.

Knock put his finger on a point and whispered. "We're here. This ladder leads to the parking garage under Hump's building."

"Will we set off any alarms going into it?"

Knock stared at the map. Alarm systems traced back and forth through the tunnels in red. He used his finger and followed one thin red line to the garage and shrugged. "There is a possibility."

"Is there any other way in?"

Knock rolled his eyes. "The front freaking door."

Logan shut the map down and started to climb. "We'll have to chance it," he said over his shoulder.

When they reached the top of the ladder Logan found a steel trap door. He pushed and nothing happened. "It's locked," he whispered to Shayna.

"Your key won't work?"

"I'll try. I've never seen a door like this." Logan took the circular disk off his neck and placed it against the steel door. Nothing happened. "Knock, are you sure this is Hump's building?"

"I can read a map, Logan. Yes, this is his building."

"Maybe it's a special complex for enforcer agents only," he hissed. "Shayna, take out the hand and let me see if his palm works. There's some kind of weird locking plate over here." He pointed to a dark-blue rectangle at the edge of the trap door. When he tapped on it, the material felt high-tech, like silicium carbide, yttrium, or zirconium ceramics. "This stuff could be from off world," he said. "I've never seen anything like it."

Shayna removed the hand from his pack. "Gross," she muttered as she handed it to him.

Logan opened the icy fingers and slapped the palm against the slick material. The door immediately slid open without a sound.

They scrambled onto the dusty concrete of the parking garage. The only vehicles in it were a few hover cars with their wheels down. Once, a long time ago, this space would have been packed with cars powered by the internal combustion engine; a mode of transportation forbidden by the Company. Logan stowed the hand in his pack with its dry-ice wrap and surveyed the garage. Banks of elevators were set into the base of the building on the other side of the open lot. "Let's go," he whispered.

"What if we set off an alarm?" Knock asked as they jogged to the elevators.

Logan grinned. "There's no fun if there's no danger."

When they got to the elevators Logan spotted another dark-blue rectangle. He leaned close to Knock. "I heard ceramic material repels human skin cells and oil. I bet that's why they used it. It never gets dirty so it can read each palm perfectly every time."

Knock took the hand out of the pack, leaving the dry ice wrapped around the severed wrist. He handed it to Logan. "Dude, we'd be nowhere without this thing."

Logan slapped the palm flat on the blue surface and lights came on indicating the elevator was moving. The whine of the super-hydraulic lift was faint and the walls barely vibrated. The door opened without a sound and they stepped inside. "What floor?" Knock asked.

"Twelve," Logan whispered.

"This feels wrong," Shayna hissed. "It shouldn't be this easy."

"Speak to the hand." Logan grinned and held up Hump's severed appendage.

"Not funny," she snapped and slapped Hump's hand. If dropped onto the floor and the three of them stood there staring at it for a minute.

"You do know the Professor's gonna try to reattach this thing when we get back."

"Oh my god, I'm so sorry," she whispered as Logan picked the severed limb up. He held it high. "Give me five."

"Disgusting," she snapped.

The elevator shot to the twelfth floor and the door slid open. Logan stuck his head into a hallway made of stainless metal and shaped like a tube. The floor was made of more of that ceramic stuff. It must have cost a fortune.

Hump's apartment was twelve ten. All even-number apartments were on the right. They trotted down the hall and stopped in front of the door. There was another dark-blue pad on the door. Logan pressed Hump's cold palm to the plate and the door slid open. Inside, lights came on, the high-tech holo-vision started up and a tall, blond, female hologram wearing a skimpy French maid's uniform greeted them.

When she bowed, her generous frontal pieces threatened to roll out of the uniform. "Holy crap," Knock said in a voice filled with awe. "Hump's got himself a hologram chick. Check out those tittle biddies."

"Welcome home, Master Humphrey," the holo-maid said. "May I prepare your favorite drink?"

"She doesn't know we're not him," Logan whispered.

"She freaking will if you tell her, dumbass," Knock said, and stepped forward. "Sure maid, fix me that drink. What's your name again? I forgot."

"I am Helga, Master Humphrey. Would you like me to add Soap to your drink as well?"

"He's a Soap addict," Shayna whispered. "Sopore and opium combined."

Knock took the lead again. "No Soap, thank you. Can you locate my level-five key? I'll be needing it shortly."

"Yes, of course, Master. It is in the safe with your other valuables. Shall I unlock it for you?"

"Yes, please do," Knock said and turned to grin at Logan. "Piece of cake."

"Did you say you wanted cake with your drink?"

"No, no, just unlock the safe and prepare the drink."

"I will need the password," Helga said in her artificially sweet voice.

Knock lifted one eyebrow and stared at Logan. Logan shrugged. He had no idea.

"Try her name," Shayna whispered.

Knock straightened his shoulders. "The password is Helga."

Helga shook her finger back and forth. "No it isn't."

Knock did more eye rolling. "Then what is it?"

"Would you like a hint?" Helga asked.

"Duh," Knock said.

"I'm sorry. I did not understand. Would you like a hint?"

"Yes, Helga, I would."

"What is your favorite day of the week?"

"Saturday," Knock snapped.

"That is incorrect. You may try one more time only."

Shayna pushed in front of Logan. "His name is Hump right?" She whispered.

Logan nodded and a light went on in his head. "The password is Hump Day."

"The safe is now open," the holo-maid said, and went into the kitchen with Enoch right behind her. Lights blinked as she turned on the food preparation system.

Somewhere in the small apartment, Logan had heard the click of a lock opening. While Knock was involved with Helga, Logan and Shayna went looking. They entered the bedroom slowly. Logan looked under the small bed as Shayna began to search the bedside table. She opened the top drawer and gasped. Logan stood up. "Is it gross? What'd you find?"

"This drawer is filled with black jelly beans."

Logan looked. There was an open bag of assorted expensive jelly beans. An inch of black beans covered the bottom of the drawer. "He must not like black ones."

"They're full of Sopore," Shayna said and opened the bottom drawer. "Now this is gross."

A porn cube sat in the bottom drawer along with Helga's controller, tissues and lotion. Logan's face burned as he slammed the drawer shut. "Sorry you had to see that."

Shayna's expression was priceless. "Which hand do you have in your pack?"

"The right one."

"You might want to make use of the hand sanitizer."

Logan choked back a snort of laughter.

Shayna shuddered. "The safe is obviously not in here."

They walked into the living room. One wall was a hologram of a forest that even smelled like fresh pines and growing things. Another wall was the holo-vision, a constant news thread ran on it with one of the Company's talking heads giving the latest news from off world. Logan watched for a minute as the newsman reported a group of miners had escaped from the Gliese diamond mine. Pictures of helos flying over a blue-green river running through waving auburn grass appeared on screen.

"Isn't that where your father is?" Shayna asked.

"I think so, but you can't be sure. It was the most active mine when he was captured."

"Maybe he's one of the escapees."

"Could be." There was no doubt in Logan's mind his father would try to escape.

He looked past the holo-vision and saw a dark-blue table. A door in the solid side of the table was ajar. "I think I found the safe," he said.

"Knock is no longer interested in our mission," Shayna said. "I think he's in love with Helga."

Logan glanced over his shoulder and saw Knock conversing with the maid. "I know what you're thinking," he called. "Don't do it."

"Don't do what?" Shayna asked as Logan squatted in front of Hump's safe and looked inside. "His mind is seldom out of the gutter," Logan said as he reached into the safe. "Bonus."

Logan pulled out the key. It was circular silver disk about three-inches in diameter. A level-seven would have been gold. He shoved Hump's severed hand with its ice pack back into his bag along with the silver key. There was a small velvet sack inside the safe. Logan opened it and poured a handful of diamonds into his palm. "Hump's been a very busy little man."

Shayna looked into the safe. "There's a book." She pulled it out and handed it to Logan.

He leafed through it and sighed. "He was keeping notes on us."

There was also a small box in the safe. Inside, Logan found two tiny zip drives. "He's probably got pictures and other stuff on these. We could have been sent to the mines or worse."

Logan shuddered and Shayna put a hand on his arm. "It's a good thing we came. When the Company finally realizes he's missing they'll check this place."

There was also a pile of plasta-tubes in the back of the safe filled with light-brown liquid. They were held together with a snap tie. Shayna pulled them out. "This is the Soap. Should we take it?"

Logan shrugged. "Might as well. I'll give it to the Professor. Maybe he can use it."

With the contents of the safe loaded into Logan's back pack, they headed for the door. Knock was sipping something out of a martini glass with Helga hovering close by. "Come on," Logan said.

"Man, Hump had it made. Why was he hanging out with Eddie in the sewers?"

"It was his job, stupid," Shayna said. "I'm sure he was ordered to do it. Jobs are how you get credit. Credit is how you afford all this stuff including the delightful and barely dressed Helga."

Knock nodded. "I knew there had to be a catch. Hey, you think I can bring Helga with me?"

Logan rolled his eyes. "No, could you please try to concentrate on getting home in one piece. Forget Helga."

Knock sighed. "That might be hard."

Chapter Twelve

They used Hump's hand to activate the elevator and begin their descent to the garage. The lift dropped like a stone and Shayna grabbed Logan's arm. She really hated elevators.

Logan patted her hand. "You'll be fine."

But they weren't. The elevator came to a sudden halt at floor five slamming them all to the floor. "What the . . .?" Knock snarled.

"We triggered something," Logan said. "We gotta deedee, man."

Knock pushed Shayna aside. "The roof."

Logan made a cup of his hands and boosted Knock high enough to reach the trap door in the roof of the car. He shoved it open, climbed up and reached back inside. "Let's go, Shayna."

Shayna was terrified. She'd always known these things were death traps.

"Go on," Logan put his hands around her waist and lifted her. She grabbed Knock's hand and he pulled her through the small door. Logan followed. The elevator shuddered.

"Quick," Knock shouted and lunged for the cables against the wall.

"Don't touch the red one," Logan yelled as he pushed Shayna toward the edge of the shaking car.

"I can't," she cried. Her heart was beating so hard she was afraid it would explode.

"You gotta." Logan shoved her off the elevator and Knock caught her arm and put her hands around the cable.

She hung there shivering. The cable was slippery. "I can't hang on."

The elevator car suddenly shot down and they were left hanging in the dark access tunnel by steel cables covered with grease. "You can," Logan whispered into her ear.

Knock had already climbed hand over hand to the floor above and knelt on a slender ledge. He reached down for her. She saw his form dimly outlined in the glow from under the door. Logan grabbed her around the waist, his arm as steely as the cable, and pushed her high enough to reach Knock's outstretched hand. When she was on the ledge, Knock turned to pry open the door. Logan swiftly clambered up beside them and helped Knock make a space large enough for them to squeeze through.

In the hallway of the sixth floor, Logan and Knock stopped long enough to check out the situation. "Front door," Logan said.

"It's our only chance," Knock turned and ran toward the door marked with a glowing red exit sign. "Shayna's got the right chip for that and you have Hump's hand. When you get the door open, I'll run through behind you. My chip might key the alarm so grab a cab as fast as possible."

Hump's hand opened the stairwell door and they thundered down the steps. At ground level, they had to use his hand again to get out of the stairwell and into the lobby. As casually as possible, Shayna and Logan walked toward the huge glass doors. Cameras hidden in each corner recorded every step they took. Ears were in every corner. Neither of them breathed. Knock hung back pressed against the stairwell door as Shayna's chip opened the locked front doors. An agent dressed in a black suit, white shirt and tie and wearing com glasses walked right by them to the elevators. Shayna could barely breathe. A solid glob of fear was lodged in her throat and she felt like she was going to throw up. Logan and Knock had reacted with speed and an amazing calmness as though things like this were expected. They hadn't hesitated a second, making snap decisions and then acting to save them.

They walked through the doors and stopped in the opening to watch the agent get on an elevator. When the doors closed behind him, Knock bolted across the pebbled blue floor and out the door. The three of them ran to the corner where Shayna held up her hand to flag one of the auto-cabs. The unmanned vehicle pulled over and the curb-side doors flew open. They piled in and Shayna looked at Logan.

"Harlem Hospital," he said as the doors snapped closed, the car's wheels went up and it shot onto Eighth Avenue.

Shayna leaned back against the plastic seat and took several deep breaths. The hover cab shot through a swarm of Company vehicles converging on Hump's building. No one paid any attention to them because only a credit disk with a lot of money behind it could activate a hover cab. She reached into her pocket and touched the six-inch leather folder containing her disk. There was no doubt it had saved them.

Logan dropped his arm around her shoulder. "You saved us," he said and gently squeezed her. "They woulda nabbed us for sure if you hadn'ta been here."

"It was all of us," she said. "We're a good team. We each have a different skill to offer. I never would have been able to get out of the elevator car without Knock's help. I was terrified."

"He can climb anything," Logan said. "That's why I shoved him out first."

Knock grinned. "Yeah, I'm a freaking monkey. Did you see that Helga? Man, I wish I had one of those."

Shayna patted Knock's leg. "You need a real girlfriend, Knock, not a holo-maid."

"I bet she does anything you tell her to," Knock said wistfully. "Anything . . ."

The cab pulled up in front of the hospital and they climbed out. Shayna stood on the curb between them unsure of where they were going or of what to do. Enoch and Logan obviously felt no such insecurity. Laughing, they headed toward the back door of the hospital. Logan stopped and grabbed her hand. "Keep up, we gotta get buried underground right now."

He pointed to the stoplights, the sides of buildings and the front of the hospital. "Cameras on us everywhere. They'll know you're with us pretty darn quick and cut off your credit. They can't mess with your chip, but you'll be as broke as us as soon as they make an ID using the facial recognition programs in all of the cameras. They'll rat you out to your parents and they could be in trouble. You crossed a line when you came with us today. There's no going back."

Shayna felt a momentary pang of fear. It seemed so slight when compared to the fear she'd felt inside the elevator. Did she love her parents? Did they love her? She really didn't know. Sopore made them so unemotional. No one hated or got violent, but there was no passion or love either. Did she want to go back to them? The answer blew into her mind with crystalline clarity. "I'm fine with that." She grabbed his hand. "There's nothing for me to go back to. I guess I'm a Vagrant now."

He pulled her by the hand into a side door of the hospital. They ducked into the first stairwell they found and went down two flights to the bottom floor. Enoch was in the lead. He stopped at the exit door and they listened. Logan nodded and Enoch opened the door. He looked up and down the long, dimly lit hall and motioned for them to follow.

They ran down the hall their feet slapping on the linoleum floor. It sounded as loud as thunder to Shayna. Shivers rolled up her spine as Logan slapped a hand-activated switch and a set of double doors opened into an incinerator that was probably also the crematorium. Enoch ran to the huge oven, opened the door and crawled through. Shayna stopped for a moment to stare into the oven, imagining all the people who had been burned to ashes inside. Logan tugged on her hand and she crawled through the huge metal doors. Logan reached behind her and slammed them shut. In seconds they were dropping into the sewer under the hospital and running for home.

When they got back to the Professor's place, Shayna remained in the shabby comfort of his living room, flopping onto the couch with a sigh of relief. Logan stood above her looking down with a slight smile on his chiseled lips. "You were freaking awesome, Shayna. We woulda been on our way to the moon right now if you hadn't come with us. You were frosty in a scary situation and that's amazing."

Logan's approval warmed her heart. She beamed up at him. "Thank you. No one's ever told me I did something good, not my parents, not school . . . well Dr. Bob, but he's like us."

Logan laughed. "Dr. Bob is like nobody I ever met. He's an original." Logan sobered. "We'd all die underground without his help. There are so few people topside like him."

Shayna nodded. "I know."

Logan walked with confidence toward the lab. He had a bag filled with goodies for Professor Goswami and the severed hand was still on ice. Diamonds and gold were the only bargaining commodities Vagrants had with topsiders. If they wanted to buy anything for the community on the black market such as chips, large pieces of equipment and expensive technological items they couldn't steal, they had to have gold or diamonds. Off-world mines had supplied the Company with these commodities which now formed the basis for the world's economy. If you wanted anything, you had to have them.

A few strange gems had been discovered off world and these were more rare and valuable but impossible to fence, the same with the new metals. Everything on the black market had to be purchased with gold or diamonds. The Professor would be so happy to see the small bag of stones Hump's safe had provided.

Professor Goswami was sitting at his desk sipping steaming hot tea when Logan and Knock burst into his lab. Hump was still out cold on the table, his wrist wrapped in dripping ice, an IV line in his left arm supplying the drugs to keep him unconscious. The Professor stood up. "I am so glad to see you are safely returned. I am hoping you brought me back his hand."

"You won't believe what we scoped at his place," Logan began.

"The hand," Prof repeated. "I need to get it back in place as soon as possible."

"Fine. I got it." Logan snagged the hand from his pack and gave it to the Professor.

"Good gracious! What did you do to it?" Professor Goswami said.

Knock coughed and grinned at Logan. "Uh, we had to use it a lot. His whole building was like palm-protected."

"Can you still put it back on?" Logan asked. He felt a little sorry for Hump. Anybody that needed a holo-maid was pretty pathetic.

The Professor unwrapped the dry-ice pack and examined the flesh around the edge of the wrist. "I will use plasti-flesh and see what I can do." He made tut tut sounds. "It's filthy and covered with some kind of gelatinous fluid."

"Mighta got a little grease on it in the lift shaft," Logan said. "And there's probably still some hand sanitizer on it."

"Should I ask why?"

Logan replied with a wry smile. "No, not really."

While the Professor examined Hump's hand, Logan dug back in his pack and pulled out the vials of Soap and the small bag of diamonds. "Can you use this stuff? The tubes contain something called Soap."

Professor Goswami placed Hump's hand on a table draped in sterile towels and took the tubes. He tilted them in the light and Logan saw particles floating in the amber liquid. "This stuff is very dangerous. No wonder our friend, here, is suffering so badly. The particular matter is heroin. I have rarely seen this much. It's worth a lot of money."

Logan hefted the bag of diamonds. "So is this. Maybe I should take some of these stones with me when I negotiate with the Tong."

"Take all of them," the Professor said.

Logan shook his head. "Naw, they got a gold bar. Eddie said they were satisfied, but I don't trust 'em. Space jackers are dangerous and, and a little cracked."

The Professor's smile was a thin line of purple lips drawn across his brown face. "I could use them to buy a better sono-scanner and there's a Da Vinci surgical robot for sale out the back door of Albert Einstein College."

Logan dumped half the stones into the Professor's hand. "Use them. I gotta bounce. It will take me at least six hours to get to Teterboro Spaceport unless I Loop."

"Is that where you will fly out of?"

Logan nodded. "Yeah, the Tong runs it."

"What Tong would this be?"

"Yee Shing."

"Oh my, you had better be careful."

"Tell me something I don't know." Logan grabbed his pack. It still contained Hump's journal and the small zip drives. "I'm gonna drop this stuff at Eddie's. Wanna come with me?" Logan asked Enoch.

Knock lifted his eyebrows. "What about your chick?"

"Shayna?"

"Dude, yeah."

"She knows I'm going."

"If you don't say good-bye to her she's gonna freak."

Logan moaned and threw his head back, eyes closed. "Man, I hate good-byes. They suck sewer scum."

"You might want to see her again, you know, and if you don't say good-bye to her, that reunion could be a little tense."

Logan laughed. "Ya think?"

Chapter Thirteen

Shayna was in the Professor's kitchen cutting up fresh vegetables. More sat in the sink in a colander.

"Did you just pick those?" Logan asked.

Startled, she looked up and into his eyes. "Yes, it's such a pleasure to walk through the hydro tanks and find squash and beans just there for the picking. I pulled some carrots, too."

"Yeah, the Professor's veggies are the best. Uh, Shayna, I, uh, I gotta bounce. Raj isn't gonna stay on the moon long, you know. They'll up ship him as soon as they get a load together. My ride to the moon leaves tomorrow."

Tears filled her eyes and leaked down her cheeks. She covered her mouth with her hand to stifle a sob. Logan moved forward as though he were on a rope attached to her. He pulled her into his arms without thinking. He hated it when women cried. "I'll be back," he whispered into her hair. "I promise."

"No, you won't. I'm never gonna see you again."

She felt so good in his arms, warm and alive. It was like nothing he'd ever experienced. He pressed his face into her hair. "I will come back. You'll see."

She tilted her head and he stared down into her heart-shaped face. "I want to go with you."

"You know you can't. Knock can't even come. The Tong only has room for one passenger and that's me."

"Then take this." She handed him a small, black leather envelope with the Company's seal embossed in the top. "You can use the Loop. I doubt if they've closed the account yet. My parents might be hoping I'll come home."

"No chance of that, huh?"

She shook her head. "I might go back to my parent's apartment just to get my stuff, but I'm happy here. I feel, I feel like I'm home."

Logan shoved the small wallet into the pocket of his black jeans. It was an amazing gift while it lasted.

She reached up and touched his face. When he felt her hand on his cheek, he kissed her. Their lips touched for one instant and he pulled away. "I can't do this, Shayna." His voice cracked. "You're tearing me up. Jeez I hate good-byes. I knew better."

She pulled out of his embrace and shoved him in the chest. "Just go then. Hurry. I'll be fine."

Logan backed away, relieved she was setting him free and horrified he might never see her again. For himself as much as for her, he grabbed her and kissed her hard. "I will be back," he said and ran out of the subway car.

Knock met him in the hallway with a crooked smile on his pasty face. "That bad?"

"Worse."

"You gonna let me go with you?"

"Can't. Only one seat on the freighter."

"Take these," Knock handed him the com glasses. He held up another pair. "Scored these off Helga the maid while you were diving into the safe. We can talk or IM."

Logan nodded and put the glasses on. They hugged briefly and Knock shoved him off. "You got a mission. Don't screw it up."

"I'll do my best. Take care of yourself and Shayna."

"You, too."

Logan headed out of the caverns taking the first tunnel to the subway. The mole rats and the Vagrants had their own watchers on all the exits. Crouched in a corner, what looked like a bundle of rags lifted a thin hand when he walked by. He waved back, turned into a side passage and went down into the sewers. He'd decided to Loop. He had Shayna's credit disk. The Loop would shoot him to Teterboro in ten minutes. Most of that time would be loading and unloading.

He ran through the dank sewers toward Eddie's, hit the canal with the torrents of fresh water, spotted the tube in the brick ceiling and the shimmery spot. He dived through it into the airlock and pounded on the door to Eddie's lab. The Asian opened it with goggles on his head and a lit welding torch in his hand.

"What'd you do with Hump?"

Logan's grin was devilish. "Had to amputate his hand."

"What?"

"We used it to get into his apartment. He lives in some agent digs with a holo-maid for company. I got you some presents while I was there."

"Place was palm-protected? What about facial recognition?"

"Palm-protected everywhere. If anything was locked with FR, we didn't run into it. Woulda sucked for Hump if we had to borrow his face."

"Yeah, really sucked. Holo-maid?"

"Oh yeah, our friend Hump is a freak." Logan pulled the journal and the box of drives out of the bag. "See if there's anything we can use in this stuff. I think he was gonna burn you." Logan handed him a sheet of paper. "The Professor wrote down a bunch of passwords and user names. Hump turned out to be very chatty."

Eddie turned off the torch and took the journal, drives and paper from Logan. "You're still going off world, aren't you?"

"Gotta bounce, man, save little Raj. The Tong is waiting."

Eddie's round face wrinkled with concern. "Watch your back with those dudes. They are . . . well the best thing I can say is they're different. Being out in space all the time must do something to them."

"What's the captain's name?"

"Chee Yong Sam or as I heard him called, Long Sam." Eddie shook his head. "He's a bad dude. Watch your back. When I paid him for you, he gave me this card and directions to a bar. Be careful."

Eddie handed Logan a business card with Chinese writing on it.

"Can you read this?" Eddie asked.

Logan laughed. "Learned to read Chinese characters before I learned to read English."

"Then you know where to go."

Logan nodded. "I'll be fine, man, or maybe I won't. I gotta give it everything though, for Raj and for us Vagrants."

The trip to Teterboro Spaceport would have been fast if the Loop went there. Logan had to take the subway to the Bronx, looking over his shoulder the whole way, where he caught the Loop to the city. Teterboro used to be a small town in New Jersey with an airport. Because of all the spaceport activity, Teterboro had grown. It had a large section of slums and tenements not usually found in Company-run cities.

Logan looked at the card Eddie had given him. It gave an address in Hackensack on Jackson Street for the Song Qingling Club. The club's name was in Chinese. The bus dropped him on the corner of Jackson and 4th Avenue in pouring rain. The neighborhood was made up of ancient twenty-first century apartment buildings, strip clubs and bars. Neon lights blinked in crazy color combinations up and down the short two blocks of the street. The brightly colored lights were reflected in the puddles.

The rusted hulks of wheeled vehicles sat parked along the curb on the right side of the street. Many were missing parts. Logan thought none looked capable of movement and wondered why they were still here. The internal combustion engine had been outlawed years ago. He leaped back in astonishment when a rusty black sedan roared to life in a crescendo of noise and black smoke. It pulled out in front of him and rattled down the street, falling into a huge pothole. Part of the back fender fell off, but the car kept going. Apparently Company laws were not well-enforced in this part of town. When he looked up and down the street, he realized there were no cameras on the buildings or the streetlights either. The Tong ruled here and the Company allowed it. That meant it was in some way profitable for them to do so.

The Song Qingling was at the end of the block. Logan stood outside the green door with a dragon painted from top to bottom for several minutes debating with himself about the merits of entering. Crude jeers, yelling and catcalls erupted from inside in a strange variety of languages. Logan gathered his courage and pushed the door open. A cloud of sweet smoke filled the large room. Loud techno music and flashing lights came from a stage where a trio of girls sang, rapped and danced in high squeaky girlish voices. Bleachers surrounding a hole in the floor took up most of the space. A long bar ran the length of the room on his left. He edged toward it while absorbing the spectacle.

There was a wide variety of customers crammed into the bleachers, all on their feet screaming. Many were Asians, but there were black, white, Hispanic and the peculiar and obvious Tong members. When he reached the bar he was able to see into the pit at the center of all the attention. A gigantic rooster, it had to be six-feet tall, was battling some kind of alien bird with a blue wattle, huge multi-colored crest and a predatory beak. The rooster was a Rhode Island Red probably raised in the Monsonta pens on growth hormones and steroids. Logan inched one butt cheek onto a bar stool as the chicken proceeded to rip into the alien fowl.

A meaty hand with tattoos across each of the knuckles fell onto the bar next to him. Logan jumped, his heart pounding. "What you want fo in here, boy?"

"I, uh, here." Logan passed the enormous bartender the card given to Eddie by Long Sam.

The bartender glanced at it and pointed to a table in a back corner so dark Logan had trouble seeing it. "You want Benny Ho. He waitin' for you. Ship ready to take off."

Logan hurried toward the table, slipped in a puddle of something he hoped was spilled beer, and caught himself on the back of the bleachers. He had to stop while two handlers toted the maimed body of the off-world bird out of the club. When the dead bird's carcass disappeared down a dark hallway, he hustled toward the table.

He stopped and gaped for a second when he saw the man waiting for him, almost changed his mind and ran. Mr. Ho looked like a Sumo wrestler. He was huge, dressed in a skintight spacer uniform which outlined every roll of blubber. His hairless dome was covered with tattooed Chinese characters and a hideous snake wrapped around his neck and disappeared under the uniform. Tattoos of a crazy off-world beast galloped across his cheeks and the bridge of his nose. He was eating spare ribs. Sauce liberally coated his hands and mouth. A greasy dollop dripped off one rubbery lip and hung suspended from a rapidly lengthening strand of saliva and sauce.

Benny Ho pointed to an empty chair. "Sit." The dollop fell to the front of Ho's shirt, slid rapidly down and disappeared.

Logan pulled the indicated chair out and perched on the edge. His backpack was pressed against the ribs of the chair back and his knees were shaking. "I'm supposed to get a ride on your ship," he squeaked.

Ho smashed a ham-sized fist covered in sticky sauce on the table. "You late, mole boy."

Logan shook his head. "I was told five o'clock and it's only four."

"When we say you late, you late. We want mo money. Long Sam say the gold you give him was already his. Got stole a long time ago, but it got his chop on the bottom. He want the rest. Now!" Ho's thick jowls flopped and flapped when he spoke and white foamy spittle formed on slabs of purple lips. His tiny, close-set eyes disappeared into nests of more flab as the alien beast running across his cheeks danced.

"I don't know what you're talking about," Logan said. "I paid all I have. I was promised a berth."

The huge man snapped his fingers and a skinny Asian, also bald without eyebrows, slammed a gold bar on the table. Ho shoved it toward Logan. He used a sausage-sized finger covered with rib sauce to point to a Chinese character on the bottom. Logan recognized the bar. It was the one he'd given to Eddie to pay with. He'd never noticed the chop. "This was part of a payment Long Sam sent to the Company seven years ago. Company never got payment. Long Sam almost lost his charter. You give me the rest right now."

Logan's hands shook as he drew the other bar out of his pack and shoved it toward Ho. "This is the only other one I have. My father left them to me."

Ho leaned forward resting his elbows on ninety-percent of the table. "Where your fadder now?"

"Gliese, the Company sent him off-world. At least I think he's on Gliese."

"You in big trouble." Ho lurched to his feet. "You go with me now, pay off yo fadder's debt."

Logan could see this interview was going to get him nowhere, especially not a spot on the Tong ship. His only chance to avoid a life of Tong servitude, which would last about six months if he was lucky, was to run. He yanked the chameleon jacket hood over his head, leaped out of the seat, dropped to his knees and scrambled into the crowd.

He heard the table crash behind him as Ho took up the chase. Logan had never been this scared in his life. He was in a strange place, didn't know the underground, didn't have an escape route planned.

The bird-fighting fans were on their feet screaming as another pair of birds entered the pit. Logan dived low and scrambled under the bleachers. He heard more crashing and screams. Ho must be chasing him. Logan was used to tight places. He belly-crawled closer to the pit. The two birds in it were more Monsonta-enhanced chickens. Logan's heart raced as he looked for a way out. He spotted a hallway heading toward the rear of the building. A waiter emerged from it carrying a tray covered with a cloth.

As Logan inched closer to it, he turned, glanced over his shoulder and screamed when Ho's meaty fist grabbed his ankle. Logan snagged his knife, a cross between an ice pick and a home-made shiv, out of his belt and jammed it into Ho's hand. Ho let go of his ankle and Logan erupted from under the bleachers, scrambling to his feet.

The betting had begun over the new bird fight. Bettors surged to their feet to exchange money all over the bleachers. Desperate, Logan shoved his way through, getting socked in the back of the head twice, yelled at and knocked around and around. For a moment, he teetered over the edge of the pit and thought he was going in. He leaped for the hallway, got hit hard by one of the fans, and shot into the pit landing on the back of a Barred Rock rooster.

He slipped off and fell to the bottom of the pit which was covered with enormous globs of chicken poop. In his entire life, Logan had never been in this dangerous of a predicament or this scared. He was functioning at a high level of genuine panic.

Above him the two roosters circled each other. One was clearly an old-school fighting cock blown up by Monsonta drugs. The other was the hormone mutant Barred Rock. Each wore metal spurs over their own huge projections, a gleaming stainless-steel beak and a hood over their combs. They squawked and crowed loud enough to deafen him as he searched for a safe corner. There wasn't one. The pit was round.

The fighting cock leaped high and raked the Rock with his spurs. Blood spurted as the Rock fought back by grabbing the fighting cock with its beak. Logan plastered himself against the wall looking for a way out. There was a rope ladder leading into the pit where the attendants descended to retrieve the birds. It was next to a lift with a sling which Logan figured they used to drag out the dead one. He edged toward the ladder. It was his only hope. That was when the two roosters spotted him. A huge golden eye rolled in his direction. The fighting cock was momentarily distracted by him. He must look like food.

The Rock saw an opening and moved in for the kill on the distracted fighting cock. Logan did the only thing he could do. He leaped on the back of the fighting cock, grabbed hold of the straps keeping the fake beak on and wrapped his legs around the muscular body. The Rock backed away from this weird combination of boy and rooster. Logan kicked the cock hard. Startled, it leaped high enough to reach the edge of the pit.

It scrabbled for purchase on the concrete-enhanced rim of the fighting pit, finally digging in and standing up. Once out, the cock crowed, flapped its wings, almost dislodging Logan, and leaped again, this time for the top of the bleachers. Fans scrambled to get out of the way. Shots were fired wildly as Logan kicked his crazy rooster again. It lifted its wings and Logan hung on for dear life by wrapping both arms around the skinny, featherless neck.

The rooster flew toward the front entrance. "Stop him. That's my bird," came from behind as the bouncer stood in front of the door with his arms out like he was going to catch the rooster. Threatened, the cock lifted both steel spurs and struck the bouncer. As gouts of blood splattered the walls, the meaty bartender emerged from behind the bar, raced to the door and flung it open. The bird spotted freedom, pecked a couple of times at the bartender and spurted through the door as a bullet smashed into the wall above them.

Logan and his feathered mount emerged into pouring rain. Logan knew the river was north. He dragged the rooster's head in that general direction and kicked it hard. His fighting cock took off down the road at a pretty good clip. The bird ran for a few yards, turned abruptly and leaped on top of one of the junker cars.

Whatever had been cloaking the car and making it resemble a rusted hulk, faded when they were on top of it, and Logan saw it was a brand new flat-black Jaguar hover car. The door clicked open and Logan dropped off his mount. The rooster flapped its wings, rose up on its legs and crowed as Logan crawled off the roof and into the leather-covered cockpit of the state-of-the-art vehicle.

The car sensed him and the door shut. Logan sat there for a minute breathing hard, catching his breath and marveling at his close escape. When his vision cleared he began to examine the interior of this insanely cool car. There was a slot in the steering wheel for a level key. Logan shrugged, pulled the level-five key out of his pack and tried it. The car activated and a female voice spoke from the dash. "Where would you like to go, master?"

"Manhattan," Logan said. The car rose, the wheels lifted and they shot by the rooster toward the river and the city. Logan looked behind and saw most of the club pouring through the green front door into the street. "Faster," he said and the car moved above the buildings and accelerated.

Logan leaned back against the plush leather which formed to his body and started deep breathing. He'd escaped but what about Raj? Riding a Tong ship to the moon was definitely out of the picture. Raj was stuck in the lunar prison with no one to help him. There was nothing Logan could do now but try for the Lift. He had the key. It was the Lift or give up on his friend, and Logan wasn't made like that. He would rescue Raj or die trying.

Chapter Fourteen

A bubble of happiness lodged in Shayna's heart. She felt giddy with joy and the excitement of new discoveries. Underground, she'd found friendship for the first time in her life and a society of people like her. The sterile existence she'd led with her parents was over. All she had to do was go home, slip into her apartment while her parents were sound asleep and collect her possessions.

"I don't think it's wise for you to return topside," the Professor told her as she washed the dinner dishes.

Shayna ignored this comment. "Do you think Logan is okay? I have a hard time imagining him shooting into space on one of the Tong's junker ships."

"They aren't all junkers. The Tong has been gathering materials and building deep space craft on their moon base. Soon, they will be a force to be reckoned with as they turn their eyes to trading and probably smuggling goods and people from the stars."

"Why does the Company allow this? Won't it endanger their monopoly on space travel?"

The Professor shook his head. "I believe they will use the Tong ships themselves and form an unholy alliance that will smother all space trade and travel for centuries. Someone must find a way to compete with them."

Shayna snorted. "And who is that gonna be?"

The Professor grinned, sat down at the table and pulled up his three-D, holographic computer screen. "People are very resourceful, Shayna. Don't count out the Vagrants or even the mole people. In New Los Angeles there is a group building a space craft as we speak. It may take a while, but we will break the hold the Company has created with their dreadful drug and by genetically altering food fed to the population. Knowledge will defeat the Company; knowledge and the indomitable human spirit." He pointed to the screen and Shayna looked. "This is video feed from underground in New Los Angeles. See the ship? It grows apace and soon will be ready to fly."

Shayna sat down opposite him. "That's wonderful and I'm proud to be a Vagrant and part of this movement, but I have to go back to my apartment. I need my clothes and, oh I don't know, my stuff."

The Professor covered her hand with his. "Don't do it, my dear. You perceive a need that does not exist. We can provide you with clothes and any other thing you wish. I feel sure you're returning topside to say goodbye to an existence you are emotionally attached to because of your youth. In your heart, you wish to make sure you make the right decision. There is no need. Stay here and wait for news of Logan."

Conflicted feelings washed through Shayna. Was he right? Did she only want to go back to her parent's apartment to make sure she didn't want to be there anymore? She stood up and grabbed her coat. "You're probably right, Professor, but it's something I have to do. What if I get back there and don't want to leave? What if I actually miss my parents?"

"What if you get back there and your parents and the Enforcers won't let you leave? Have you thought of that? I'm sure they know about your trip to Humphrey's home and the subsequent escape. They could be setting a trap for you."

Shayna shrugged off the Professor's concerns. "My parents would never do that to me. They might be cold and bombed on Sopore, but they'd never sell me out to the Company."

The Professor tut tutted. "Don't be so sure. The Company can put a lot of pressure on them to obey their dictates." He stood up, took her hands and smiled gently. "I see you are determined. Take these so you can communicate with us." He handed her a pair of the com glasses used by all Enforcers and now adopted by the Vagrants.

She took them and slipped them on. Immediately a voice spoke into her ear. "Who's wearing the glasses?"

"It's me, Knock, Shayna. The Professor gave them to me."

"Why'd he do a fool thing like that?"

Shayna snorted. "It's not a foolish thing. I'm going topside to collect some of my belongings. I came here only with my purse and the clothes I was wearing. The Professor wants me to have a com device in case I run into trouble."

"You should wait until daylight," Knock said.

"No, my parents will be zonked on the Sopore load they get from drinking their evening glass of wine. It'll be safer at night. Fewer Enforcers."

"That's what you think," he mumbled. "Don't do it, Shayna."

"Who are you speaking to?" the Professor asked.

"Knock," she whispered. "He doesn't want me to go. He says it's too dangerous."

The Professor's eyebrows went up. "When a wild child such as Enoch says a thing is dangerous, do you not question your intentions?"

Shayna shrugged off his restraining hand. "I have to do it, Professor. I won't be happy here until I say goodbye to that life."

She left filled with misgivings. As she walked out of the populated areas and into the darkness, her stomach churned. Was she wrong?

The Professor had drawn a map for her. Shayna carefully followed the directions written in his neat handwriting. When she arrived at the subway station close to her home, it was deserted. The empty kiosks, waiting areas and trains filled her with foreboding. She'd never been down here this late. It was after midnight. The well-ordered citizens of the Company were all sleeping. She felt exposed as she walked across the vast and open and empty waiting area, through the exit turnstile and onto the escalator leading to the street.

She kept her head bowed with the hood of her jacket pulled over her hair. Cameras blinked green as they picked up her presence. Terror at being caught filled her and once again, she doubted her decision to go home. What if this was a trap and the Professor right?

She rushed out of the tunnel and onto the deserted streets of Harlem. She fought the urge to run. That would surely excite interest among those who monitored the cameras. When she reached the door of her apartment building, it opened. She raced into the foyer and toward the lobby elevators with her heart pounding. The elevators opened as she approached and she rushed inside. Her chip told the elevator exactly at which floor to stop. She shifted anxiously as it whisked her to her floor. When the doors opened, she peered into her hallway. All was quiet and she sighed with relief.

Her fears were unfounded and it was just as she'd told the Professor. Everyone was asleep. Her door opened when she approached. This should have warned her. It usually required her to order it to open. In the back of her mind, she figured it was because of the hour and her lengthy absence, but when she stepped inside, she saw her family's apartment swarmed with Enforcers.

Horror froze her for one moment then she wheeled around and ordered the door to open. "No, Ms. Nagata, you may not egress the apartment."

A female enforcer wearing a black skirt and jacket approached her. Her parents stood in the background with a confused expression on their faces. "Mom! Dad! Stop them." She keyed the comm. glasses. "Knock, they have me."

"Who is she, Donald?" Her mother asked her father.

"I have no idea, my dear, but don't worry, the Enforcers will take care of the intruder."

Shayna broke away from the enforcer holding her arm and ran to her parents. "Mother, don't you know me. It's Shayna, your daughter."

The glasses crackled in her ear, but she heard no voice only static. They must be damping the signal.

Her mother's face reflected a moment's confusion and she looked at her husband. He put a comforting arm around his wife's shoulders." I don't know who you are, but you have no business in this apartment."

Shayna burst into tears as the female enforcer dragged her out of the apartment. She tore at the restraining hand. "You can't do this to me. I live here."

"Be quiet, Miss, or we'll have to tranquilize you. You'll wake the residents." The female agent grabbed her com glasses off her face. "You won't be needing these where you're going."

Shayna shrieked with fury and fear and fought the woman like a tigress. The woman struggled to shield her face and hold Shayna at the same time. Two agents approached her from behind. She felt a sharp pain in her neck and Shayna's fear and desperation evaporated. She hung in their grip like a zombie, unaware of anything but a dull buzz in her brain with tears running down her face.

Logan left the fancy hover car behind a restaurant on Lenox and hit the tunnels. His mind turned over different ideas and possibilities for saving Raj. The Lift was now his only option. He had four more days until the moon was out of range and the Lift shut down, so he had to make a new plan in a hurry.

As he hustled down tunnels and through the subterranean maze he called home, he thought about Shayna and smiled. Since he wasn't hurtling toward the moon on the Tong's ship, he could see her again. He immediately frowned. She'd want to come with him to the moon. She was terrified of elevators, but she would brave them to help rescue Raj. It would be hard to say no.

Logan had never had a girlfriend before. He'd never kissed a girl before. Vagrants like him lived on the edge, always running and hiding from the Enforcers. He'd never had the time or the opportunity to meet girls. Shayna had come out of the blue. She'd hunted for him, found him and he had to admit, he liked her.

He passed what looked like a pile of rags. An arm shot out of it and waved. The mole people made great sentries. He ran down the Professor's corridor and rapped once on the blue door before pushing inside. He couldn't wait to see Shayna and tell her about his meeting with the Tong and the giant roosters.

The Professor greeted him with dismay. "Logan, why have you returned?"

"Long story. Where's Shayna? I don't want to tell it twice."

An aura of unease radiated from the Professor. He sat at the little table and hovered over a cup of tea. "She went to her home to gather some possessions."

"What?" Logan glanced around the subway car. "You're kidding, right?"

"No, my son, she insisted she had to go back to her apartment. She said it was to get clothes and other things she needed, but was induced to admit it was partly to reassure herself that she was making the right decision."

"They'll pick her up, Professor." Logan grabbed his head as he sank into a chair opposite the Professor. "This is a disaster. I can't believe you let her go."

"I tried to stop her. She was adamant. What happened with the Tong?"

"They wanted more money. I don't think they ever had the intention of giving me a berth. They said my gold brick had been stolen from them and demanded the remaining bricks. I had to run for my life. They were planning to conscript me."

The Professor shook his head as he sipped his tea. "That would have been the end for you."

"Don't I know it. I had to run for my life on the back of a fighting cock." Logan filled the Professor in on the remaining details of his adventure while he made himself a cup of tea. When he'd finished his story, he got up and paced. "Why'd you let her go?"

"I was unable to convince her of the error in her logic."

"How do I rescue Raj now?" Logan fell back into his chair. "Shayna is gone, I have no way to get to the moon. I'm so screwed."

"Do not despair. There is always the Lift. You have a key. Why don't you talk to your friend Eddie about the technological details of the Lift and see if there are weakness in the procedure or a way to get on board without being seen."

Logan leaped to his feet again and began pacing. "I will. But I'm worried about Shayna. How long has she been gone?"

The Professor examined his tea cup. "Too long."

Chapter Fifteen

Shayna stared at the other girls in her cell with dead eyes. In a few minutes, they would all be loaded into the Lift and sent to the moon. There were very young girls, some only seven or eight, and grown women. They were all healthy and attractive which worried her. The cell was so packed, she could only huddle on one of the benches crammed between a girl of ten named Cressida, Cressy for short, and a big woman wearing Vagrant clothing.

Cressy pressed against Shayna for comfort and looked up at her out of huge dark eyes. "What's going to happen to us?"

"I'm not sure, little one. I know we're going on the Lift to the moon. After that, it's anyone's guess. I've never been, you know."

Cressy tucked her hand in Shayna's. "I'm afraid."

"Me too. I hate elevators."

The Vagrant woman looked across Shayna at Cressy. "Wherever we're going, they'll shove their poison infected food on us. Don't eat it."

Shayna's eyes flew open. "I can't eat it. I'm allergic to corn."

"Then I wouldn't worrit about the Lift cause you'll die in the pens else. Sure as I'm from underground, they'll force you to eat. They want us all nice and sedated. We be so much easier to abuse that way, you see."

"That's a comfort," Shayna said. "No matter what, I'm dead."

Two guards opened the door and motioned for the women to move out. "Form two lines," a heavy-set man in the tan uniform of Company employees said. "He removed a snack cake from his pocket and took a huge bite. "Hurry, we got a schedule to keep."

The women hustled down the corridor between empty cells. Theirs had been the only occupied one. Apparently, the Company was having trouble filling their quotas. A rumble vibrated the floor beneath their feet and Shayna sobbed with fear.

"It's okay, Miss Shayna," Cressy said. "I'll hold your hand."

Shayna tried to smile. "Thanks, little one. I can use a hand right now."

"You're very scared. Even I can see that."

"I told you, I've been terrified of elevators my whole life."

"Maybe you always knew you'd make this trip. You know, inside yourself, like a premonition."

"That's a big word for a little girl."

Tears filled Cressy's eyes. "My mommy taught me to read and gave me lots of books."

"Where are you from?"

Cressy waved her hand to indicate far away. "I lived on a farm in the country. It was a real big farm. My mommy got in the family way without a permit and we ran away."

Shayna glanced down at the child. Should she even ask? "Where's your mommy?"

The girl looked down and clung to Shayna's hand with a steely grip. "I don't know."

The corridor ended at a set of metal doors. They opened smoothly and the women filed into a small airlock. As the doors shut, Shayna's heart pounded in her ears. The women were compressed into the small space shoulder to shoulder. Some of the younger girls began to cry. The women all looked at the walls and the door leading out the other side with fear in their eyes.

Jets of air whooshed out of the wall filled with some kind of antiseptic spray. Shayna recognized the smell from her time at the hospital. The spray coated them for at least a full minute then stopped and the exit doors opened. More guards waited on this side, different ones. The guards carried hot shots, sticks with electricity-charged barbs on the end like cattle prods. They pushed the women down a narrow tunnel leading down. Yellow lights set inside metal cages cast a sickly glow on the women who looked terrified as they trotted down the tunnel.

At the end of the tunnel, the vibrations in the floor increased. A huge capsule set inside a shimmering tube waited at the end. The women were shoved inside, between rows of seats to a door and a set of stairs. They filed down the stairs and emerged into another chamber with more seats. These were narrow and form-fitting. Everyone took a seat and buckled a safety harness across their bodies.

Shayna could barely breathe. Her fear threatened to overcome her. She buckled her harness and giggled. Cressy looked at her with a question in her eyes. "Sorry," Shayna whispered. "I was just laughing because we're buckling these belts on. As if they will help if anything goes wrong."

"Don't say that," Cressy said, her dark eyes grave. "We'll be safe. They send this thing back and forth a hundred times a day."

"I know," Shayna squeaked. "I'll be fine. Ignore me."

The doors clanged shut and cold air filled the cabin. The vibrating they'd felt under their feet increased until Shayna could feel it in her bones. A scream not unlike the Loop built in machinery somewhere outside the capsule. Shayna clenched her teeth and gripped Cressy's hand and the arm rest. This was it.

A sudden lurch, her stomach dropped worse than any elevator she'd ever been in, and a huge weight fell on her chest pressing her into the seat. Cressy's grip tightened as Shayna felt her lips pull away from her face and her ears pop. They must be shooting to the moon right now through the electromagnetic tube known as the

Lift. Shayna was too afraid to cry. She knew this lasted for an hour and wondered if any of them would survive it.

When hours passed and Shayna did not return, Logan started pacing the floor. "Pacing will not help you," the Professor noted as he slowly rose and began washing the cups.

"I can't sit still. Shayna could be dead, Professor. Doesn't that bother you?"

"I don't believe the Company would waste a young woman. They need warm bodies to populate their new mining towns and to work the mines. I heard the one-child law has been set aside so more conscripts can be bred."

"I don't care about that, Professor. All I care about is Shayna. What should I do?"

"It seems as though you have formed an attachment to the young woman."

Logan stopped pacing. Had he? He knew he cared about her, but how much? "Maybe I have, but what do I do about it? Do you think she liked me? What if she just went home? Maybe being a Vagrant didn't work for her."

"Listen to your heart, young man. I cannot advise you. I believe she would not go home. I think she was truly attached to you and to us. But this puzzle is not for me to untangle. I am going to bed. I cannot be up all night worrying. That occupation is for the young."

Logan, even though exhausted, couldn't imagine sleep when he didn't know where Shayna was. Even though the Professor didn't think so, maybe she had decided life as a Vagrant wasn't for her. He kept seeing her strapped into a seat on the Lift screaming and screaming. Unable to stand the waiting any longer, Logan went hunting for Knock. He found his friend sleeping in his room behind the Professor's lab.

Hump was in a cell next to the lab, sleeping. His wrist and hand were bandaged. The Professor had reattached the hand while he was gone. Logan knocked on Knock's door and got no answer so he shoved it open. His friend sat up and rubbed his eyes. The incomparable Helga sat on a bench watching. She stood up when Logan entered and curtsied. "How may I serve you?"

"You're kidding?" he said to Knock.

Knock grinned. "I had to go back for her," he said. "I couldn't leave her behind."

"How'd you get in to rescue her?"

Knock threw his legs over the edge of the bed. "You're not the only one with tricks. What the heck are you doing here? I thought you'd be on a space ship headed for the moon by now."

"The Tong aren't to be trusted."

Knock snorted. "Duh! So what's the new plan?"

"I can't think about it right now. Shayna's missing."

"Well you better think about it. The Lift will shut down in four more days and they'll be firing Raj into outer space any minute."

"I know, I know, but I gotta find Shayna."

Knock pulled a small black box out from under his bed and waved his palm over it. Helga immediately disappeared. "I'm up. Let's go look for her."

"Maybe we can think of a plan to get on the Lift while we do it," Logan said. "Let's go see Eddie. We can get him to check the list of transportees for Shayna's name. It'll save a bunch of time. I'm not real excited about going to Shayna's digs. If she's been picked up, the Enforcers will be swarming the place."

"Good thinking."

Logan nodded. "And Eddie might have an idea for getting on the Lift without detection, too. I got a feeling I'm going to be taking a long ride soon."

They passed Hump's cell on the way out. He was thrashing around on his cot moaning for Helga. "Where is she?" he wailed. "My Helga. I need her."

Logan stepped close to the bars. "Wake up, Hump. You're having a nightmare. Helga's got a new man and you're a prisoner of the Vagrants."

Hump sat up and Logan was stunned by the man's appearance. He looked ten years older and he'd lost at least twenty pounds.

"I need a soda or a Twinkie. Come on guys, please for the love of God."

Logan shook his head. "You'll be better off without Sopore."

Hump held up his hand. "Says who? You owe me. Look what that butcher did."

"The Professor will take good care of you," Knock said. "He's a straight up guy."

"Sure he will, as long as he don't need my hand for anything else."

"I think you're safe there," Logan said. "And you'll be better once you're off Sopore."

"I don't wanna be off Sopore. Helga! I need a Twinkie." Hump screamed. "Please, I'm dying."

Shayna was too weak to stand when the Lift screamed to a shivering stop. The capsule's vibrations didn't cease, but the capsule no longer moved. Cressy had to unbuckle her safety harness. When the catch released she fell out of the seat and patted her arms and face. "I'm safe," she sighed. "All of me made it."

Cressy giggled. "Did you think part of you would get lost?"

Shayna slowly stood up. "The thought had occurred. I was pretty scared."

A guard entered the cabin and pointed to Shayna. "Get off the floor."

Shayna wobbled to her feet and faced the guard. Her stomach churned, she burped, bent over and projectile vomited across the guard's feet. He leaped out of the way, but not in time. Disgusted, he banged his boots to clean them, grabbed her shoulder and shoved her toward the door. "Get in line," he snarled.

Cressy took her hand. "You okay?"

"I am now," Shayna said with a smile.

The guard quickly marshaled the captives up the stairs. They exited the capsule emerging into an atrium made completely of glass. The ceiling soared a hundred feet above them. Plants grew in profusion, including tall palm trees. Shayna stopped to stare out of the windows. Earth in all its blue and green glory rotated through black velvet sprinkled with shiny lights. It seemed close enough to touch. The barren moonscape surrounded them. A concrete structure was just visible off to the side of the huge welcome center. The atrium was the entrance to the moon center where all passengers of the Lift that weren't going to jail were greeted.

The guard grabbed her arm. "That's enough gawking. This ain't a guided tour."

He shoved her ahead of him. They walked across marbled floors and through a sliding door that opened silently. The doors led to another long hallway. At the end was an airlock made of gray metal. Shayna knew they were on the moon, but it seemed fantastic. The corridors were the same as the ones on earth. If she hadn't seen Earth through the glass she'd think they were still there. It was as though they'd never left.

When they were through the airlock, they started a long march through narrow passages that went on forever. They walked and walked until Shayna felt like she was going to collapse. One of the women did and was quickly picked up and put on a moving trolley. By the time they reached their destination, a low-ceilinged open room filled with hundreds of women, there were four women on the trolley.

The doors clanged shut behind them and Shayna looked around. There were rows of empty cots. This facility was set up for many more women than were in it. The large holding chamber was carved out of solid rock. The ceiling was raw stone with marks where machinery had tunneled into it.

She walked down the rows of cots until she found a secluded one in a corner and fell onto it. Cressy sat on one next to hers, and the Vagrant woman, whose name turned out to be Grace, sat on one next to Cressy's. A pile of clothing was neatly folded in the middle, a gray onesie and gray boots along with gray underwear.

Shayna picked up a pair of briefs. "You think they chose gray so when they get old and discolored no one will know?"

Cressy shrugged. "I think they chose gray so we would blend into the walls."

Shayna smiled wanly and looked at the women already in the containment facility. They seemed well-fed. All were dressed in the gray onesie. They crowded around the newcomers looking for news of loved ones back on Earth. When Shayna felt recovered enough to move, she headed for a knot of women near a water dispenser. She took a paper cup and filled it, drinking thirstily. A woman who appeared to be in her forties moved closer to Shayna.

She waited for Shayna to finish her water and smiled. "I'm Deena. Where you from?"

"New Washington," Shayna said. "How long have you been here?"

Deena sighed. "I keep hoping to meet someone from New L.A. The Vagrant population there is righteously good at protecting its people. Not many get captured. I've been here for three weeks."

Shayna looked around. "And the rest of you?"

"The longest resident has been here a month. I heard we're gonna to be shipped out soon."

Shayna moaned. "Oh no. Do you know how soon?"

Deena shook her head. "We think they want to fill this pod. It's only about two thirds of capacity."

Shayna hoped Logan would make it to the moon to save Raj, but he wouldn't know she was here. No one would. No one was coming to save her. Going back to her home was so dumb. Tears rolled down her face. She would never see Logan again. He might be in the pod next to this one saving Raj, but he would never know she was here.

Deena took her arm. "You okay?"

Shayna nodded. "Just a delayed reaction I guess. Do we ever get to see the male detainees?" Maybe she could find Raj if they were allowed to mingle.

"Mess is a coed deal. We eat with the dudes three times a day in a giant cafeteria."

Hope blossomed in Shayna's heart. "I imagine we're watched pretty closely."

Deena grinned. "Yeah, but the guards are human and they know we got needs."

Shayna's eyebrows flew up. "Needs?"

Deena gouged her with an elbow. "Yeah, you know, you meet a guy you like, there's ways to be alone."

Chapter Sixteen

Logan and Knock slipped through Eddie's airlock and into the lab. Eddie was playing with his pet Sniffer. He looked up and grinned. "Check this out. I rigged it to sniff out Sopore."

Eddie put an open can of soda on the table and used the remote to activate the Sniffer. It wobbled to its feet and then scrabbled around the room investigating all of them. It climbed the table and found the can. A siren went off and Eddie laughed like a crazy man. "It can detect even small amounts so when it finds an enforcer underground or someone you think is cool, it can sniff them and tell you if they're on the drug."

Logan nodded. "Very cool, Eddie, but we got bigger problems. We think, but we're not sure, the Company's got Shayna."

"Who?"

"The Topsider girl who came down to the levels to be with me."

Eddie laid down the remote. "This the first I ever heard of her. I thought you were taking a long space ride on a Tong ship."

"The gold my dad left me was stolen from the Tong. They wanted it *all* back. I barely escaped being conscripted as a Tong galley slave by a Tong member who looked like a sumo wrestler."

"Bad deal that. You'd be dead within a year."

"Know it. Is there a way to hack into the camera feed for her apartment? Going there would be a very bad idea if she's been taken. I'm thinkin' checking the cameras would be the easiest way to make sure she didn't just decide to go home."

Eddie nodded. "Sure. Give me the address."

Logan told him and they sat down at Eddie's biggest computer station. He opened a browser and did a lot of typing. An array of camera feeds came up. Eddie blew each one up, finally choosing one. "This looks like the right address."

Logan leaned forward. "Holy crap! The place is crawling with Enforcers."

Knock whistled. "Good damn thing we didn't decide to go there."

"I had a bad feeling," Logan said, and leaned back in his chair. "At least we know she didn't throw us under the bus. For a minute, I thought maybe she went home for good. Eddie, can you check the lists? Her name's Shayna Nagata."

"What you gonna do now, Loge? How you gonna get to the moon?"

Logan shrugged. "I got a Level-Five key. I'll think of something." He paused thoughtfully. "You know where I can get a spacesuit?"

Eddie sat down and cued the giant screen to come on. It shimmered in the air and then presented them with a list of detainees in green against a black background. The names scrolled past rapidly. When Eddie came to the Ns he slowed it and scanned them. "Here," he said and pointed to a name. "She was transported yesterday evening."

Eddie leaned back in his chair. "Dude, if you're thinking about the Lift, it's got three more days and then it's gone."

Logan rolled his eyes. "I know that. What about the space suits?"

Eddie pursed his lips and tapped them with his forefinger. "Let me think. You can order new ones online from Wal-Mart, but they're really expensive. I don't know anyone but the Tong who uses them. They're not something you find on the street."

Logan pulled out Shayna's wallet containing her credit disk. "If this still works, we're golden. Can you order them for pickup from a scrambled IPO?"

Eddie grinned. "Gimme that thing."

Eddie turned the disk over in his hands. "How much you think this has on it?"

"Shayna made me think it was unlimited."

Logan pulled up a chair and watched as Eddie opened a new window on his browser and searched for spacesuits on the Wal-Mart site. Wal-Mart was the only retailer left in the U.S. The Company owned it. If you wanted to buy something, you ordered it from them and it was delivered to your home by drone. Only Logan and Eddie didn't have a home.

Eddie found the suits and whistled. Wow! Quite expensive." He tried to buy them for pickup and the site balked. "They're saying the suits have to be delivered."

Logan thought for a moment. "What about the shop? You do have one up there." He pointed.

Eddie thought about it. "I could do that."

He went back to the computer and ordered the suits, then he continued to a new window and started typing furiously. "What're you doing now?" Logan asked.

"Trying to keep this credit disk active forever."

Logan whistled and leaned closer to watch the screen. "You can do that?"

Eddie pushed his face away. "Yeah, maybe, if I don't have people hanging over my shoulder."

An alarm clanged inside the store above them. Eddie pointed. "Your suits are here."

"Already?"

"The distribution center is in Harlem."

Knock went up and returned lugging the two suits. "Got 'em," he said.

Eddie had finished fiddling with Shayna's credit information. He leaned back in the chair and stared at Logan out of his slanted eyes. "So, what's your plan?"

Logan pulled out the silver disc he'd found in his father's stash and keyed the blueprint. "I need to find the back door of Palin Penitentiary."

Eddie got a magnifying glass, flopped onto his hands and knees and began searching under the three-D image, and on each side. He looked at every crack and crevasse, finally sitting back on the floor. "There are two construction entrances. I can tell you how to get to them, but fact is they could be blocked up. There's no guarantee they're open or in working order."

Logan nodded. "Are there any service entrances?"

Eddie pointed to three obvious ones. "There's one from the spaceport here. There's another leading to an underground service tunnel system beneath the prison that also goes to the Hilton. Then there's this one which I think goes to the landfill."

"Wherever we go, we leave garbage," Logan said.

Eddie climbed back into his chair. "True. So, do you have a plan?"

Logan walked around the small room picking up tools, examining Eddie's various projects. "I was hoping you'd have some ideas. How can I get on the Lift without being noticed?"

Eddie nodded. "Let's do like we did with the prison. I think the Lift has basic design plans online. I'll pull them up."

The three of them crowded around Eddie as the skeleton of the Lift appeared on the big screen in front of him. Eddie rotated it and they all examined it carefully. Finally Logan pointed. "This service area in the nose looks possible, but we have to get by the guards. I have a key to get inside, but we can't be walking around looking like Vagrants."

"Vagrants wearing space suits," Knock snorted. "That won't alert anyone."

"The space suits are okay as long as you have a face that gets by the facial recognition program guarding the service areas," Eddie said. He pointed to two symbols on the Lift design. "They just installed the system according to this notation."

Logan shook his head. "We're screwed."

"Too bad we can't use Hump's face," Knock said.

Eddie scratched the thin beard sprouting on his chin. "You just gave me an idea, Knock." He got up and pointed to a piece of equipment Logan had been examining only minutes before. "This is a three-D printer. It can copy anything and create it in plastic."

Logan shrugged. "I don't get it."

Eddie began pulling up the camera feed from Shayna's apartment. "If it can reproduce anything, maybe it can reproduce faces."

Logan rolled a chair closer to Eddie. "No way."

They scanned enforcer faces for ten minutes finding only two full faces; a woman and a black man. "If this works," Logan said to Knock. "You're the woman. I have no problem being a black dude."

"Why do I have to be the woman?" Knock complained.

"You're skinnier than me and you have those blond dreads."

"Not fair."

Eddie sent the faces to the printer and they waited for it to produce. The smell of hot plastic filled the small room as the printer buzzed, an alarm sounded and the printer burped. Eddie got up and fished in the tray under the printer. He held up a plasti-flesh mask the spitting image of the black enforcer. "You have to cut out the eye holes," he said. "But, otherwise, it's perfect."

The printer burped again and Eddie retrieved the mask of the female enforcer. He handed it to Knock. "I hope this works. They look good enough to me."

Logan formed the mask to his face. It clung to the contours. "You're right. This may do the trick."

Knock stared at Logan. "Dude."

"What?"

"Did you see the chick on the tapes? She had, like, monster boobs."

Logan looked at Eddie. "Can your printer do boobs?"

Eddie grinned. "We shall see."

A few minutes later, the machine burped and out popped two perfectly shaped breasts made of plasti-flesh and rubber. Knock pulled them out of the tray and held them up to his chest. "What do you think?"

Logan rolled his eyes. "I think we're nuts."

Chapter Seventeen

Deklan Hall climbed the rust-colored ridge with Cain Hollyroad right behind him. Helos had buzzed their encampment two days in a row and Dek feared the Company was alerted to their presence and planned an attack. The helos had flown low as though on a mission. They didn't circle or set down. Dek had to get to the bottom of this new activity to ensure the safety of his people.

"I hope we can see where they were coming from once we're at the top," he said to Cain.

"I can't believe they didn't see us. I mean, there was smoke coming out of Maria's chimney."

"I got a feeling there's something over this ridge," Dek said. "It's like we're now on a flight path of some kind. I'm worried, man. If that's true, we'll have to move. They might not have spotted us yet, but they will."

The ridge led to another higher ridge. Climbing was easy on Gliess. Dek sucked in the oxygen-rich air and bounded up the crumbling slope with ease. The fetid stench of a loris filled his nostrils and he stopped. "Smell that?"

Cain nodded. "Close."

The loris was a giant poisonous lizard-like creature that inhabited the heights of Gliese. It spit on its enemies blinding them, but its meat was tasty and its hide made vests and pants that lasted forever. The two men slowed and crept closer to an outcropping of striated red, blue and rust-colored stone. The smell got stronger and Dek took out his blaster. Cain was armed only with a compound bow he'd crafted from local wood. He knocked a bolt as they leaped over the edge of the cliff and raced around the outcropping.

The loris crouched in front of a cave tearing apart a hopper. It lifted its flat head and hissed. Chunks of hopper flesh fell out of its mouth as Dek stepped back and let Cain take the shot. Blaster charges had to be saved if possible and used in emergency situations only.

The bolt hit the loris between its spinning red eyes. Purple goo spurted out of the hole and the lizard dropped onto the dead hopper. "Amazing shot," Dek said as he walked over to the loris and pulled the bolt out of its head. "We should gut it before we go or its poison will ruin the meat.

"I'll do it. You climb up the ridge and see what's over there."

Dek nodded, scrambled up the last thirty feet to the top of the mountain and used his field glasses to scan the valley below. What he saw blew his mind. He turned and shouted down to Cain. "You gotta see this, man. There's spaceships down there."

Cain finished removing the lizard's strange internal organs and scrambled up the hill. The two of them stared in shock at the busy encampment below. Two battered space craft rested beside a temporary structure and a tent city. "Who are they?" Cain asked.

Dek used the glasses to examine each ship. "They aren't Company ships and they don't belong to the military. They look like flying junk yards. Some of the parts are different colors and appear to be tacked on."

"Aliens?"

Dek snorted. "I don't think so. The Company knows they're here so they have to be affiliated in some way or they'd be burning them out as we speak."

Cain crouched beside Dek and took out his own glasses. He sighted something Dek had missed and pointed. "Is that a sumo wrestler?"

****

A bell sounded inside the open women's pod. Deena grabbed Shayna's hand. "Dinner."

"Come on," Shayna said to Cressy. "It's time to eat. Remember what I told you about avoiding certain foods."

"Why?" Cressy said.

"Because the Company poisons the food. Just watch me and do what I say."

The women lined up in two columns and slowly passed through double doors leading into a huge cafeteria filled with the smell of green beans and grease. Long tables filled most of it. Shayna craned her neck to see the other side where the men were filing through their door. She remembered Raj as being small with brown skin and black hair and she hoped she'd recognize him after only seeing him that one time. It had been a stressful situation so maybe his image was imprinted on her memory.

The line moved slowly. Some of the women broke off and ran to be reunited with a man from the other section. The food smelled like it was full of Sopore. Shayna was terrified of eating it accidentally and becoming deathly ill.

There were two feeding stations, one on each side of the enormous chamber. Shayna grabbed Cressy's hand and pulled her toward the other side of the room. Most of the men had lined up at the far station and she wanted to be there. The floor of the cafeteria was gray tile, dark gray. The onesies were gray and the walls were gray. Only the faces of the detainees showed any color. Shayna scanned each one looking for the dark face of Raj.

When they reached the food station, she pulled a metal tray off a shelf and handed it to Cressy along with a plastic-wrapped set of eating utensils. The package contained chopsticks, a spoon, a napkin and salt and pepper packets. The cafeteria workers were all men. When Shayna examined them closely, she realized they were wearing the gray jumpsuit of the detainees. It made sense that the Company would use them instead of actually paying real people.

She eyed the offered food with suspicion. There was nothing fresh. Everything looked like it had been dumped out of a can or fried probably in corn oil. Shayna began to fear she would starve. She leaned across the serving line. "Excuse me, I'm allergic to corn. What can I eat?"

The man she spoke to wore a long gray beard, had pock-marked cheeks and round blue eyes that seemed to be always opened at their widest. When he shook his head and shrugged Shayna despaired. One of the guards saw her trying to speak to the servers and pushed his way into line. "What's the problem?"

"I can't eat anything with corn in it," she said with a trembling voice. "I'm allergic."

He pointed to a serving pan filled with gray spotted beans. "They're safe."

Cressy was holding out her plate for one of the men to fill with fried meat cakes. "What about that?"

The guard shook his head. "It's soy, but there's corn flour in them, too."

Shayna grabbed Cressy's hand and jerked her plate away. "No, it's bad for you."

Cressy's soft brown eyes filled with tears. "But I'm hungry and I don't like beans."

Shayna didn't know what to do. When she looked around, all the people had the familiar Sopore stare. Keeping the child off it would be almost impossible. She relented, but made Cressy take a large portion of the beans. Maybe if she didn't eat much of the Sopore rich food, she would be okay. When they reached the dessert, an orange gelatin filled with canned fruit, she saw Raj. He was collecting dirty trays and lugging them back to the dishwashing area.

Shayna handed Cressy her tray. "Take this to a table and wait for me."

Cressy looked surprised but did as she was told while Shayna ambled to the tray and dish drop off area. She waited nervously as she scanned the entire room for guards. Raj emerged from the dish area shuffling along with his head down. Shayna stepped forward. "Raj!" she hissed.

Startled, he looked up. When he didn't see anyone he recognized he shrugged and moved to the huge bus tubs of dirty dishes.

"Raj!" Shayna raised her voice a notch.

When he realized it was her speaking to him, his black eyebrows rose, but he made no move in her direction. She soon realized why when a large hand grabbed her elbow. "You trying to cause trouble?" A gruff voice demanded.

Shayna pushed his hand away. "No, I just thought I knew him . . . from home, you understand."

"Move along," he snarled. "We might allow fraternization, but we don't promote it."

Shayna balked. "I really need to talk to him. He's my, uh, he's my little brother."

"I told you move along." This time the guard's voice was low and ominous, but Shayna was afraid she'd never see or find Raj again before it was too late.

"Please, sir. I haven't seen him in weeks and my Mom told me to find him." She leaned around the guard and screamed. "Raj!"

Raj dropped the trays he was carrying with a loud clatter and turned around. He stared at Shayna with his mouth open and his eyes wide with fright. Shayna pulled away from the guard, darted around him and leaped over the long metal table holding the dirty trays. She pushed a giant black trash can over and ran through the dish room door. Raj stood watching her frozen with terror. When she grabbed him in a huge hug, she whispered into his ear in a low urgent voice. "Logan sent me. He's on his way here to save us . . . I hope."

Before Raj could answer, the guard grabbed her shoulder and jerked her off her feet. She fell to the wet floor and lay there staring up at Raj and the angry guard. "You are going into the isolation pod," he snarled as he grabbed her arm and jerked her to her feet. He put his big hand under her elbow and Shayna only had time to shoot Raj a look of entreaty over her shoulder before he hustled her away.

****

Logan examined himself in the mirror. He wore the face of the black SS agent and the tight hood of the space suit. The mask was flipped up and ready to drop over his face if needed. But the service personnel for the Lift would think it odd if he walked around with the glass covering his face.

He adjusted the mask slightly to cover some white skin by his ear and pulled his hair out of the hood to help cover it. "Think this will work?" he asked Eddie.

Eddie was staring with extreme fascination at Knock. Knock had his fake boobs in place, his female mask on and his hair combed out into long scraggly lengths. "Not bad," Eddie mused. "Not bad at all. I might even ask you out."

"Back off," Knock said. "I wouldn't date you if you were the last man on earth."

Logan put his hands on his hips and examined Knock. His space suit of form-fitting silvery material looked fine. The air packs on his back were right, but there was something missing. Then it hit him. "Badges, we need badges."

Eddie nodded. "You are so right. You'd be stopped in a heartbeat. Back to the tapes."

After scrolling through the video feed from the apartment, Eddie was able to get good photos of the agent's badges. He sent them to his printer and waited. The machine burped and out came two perfect badges. Eddie provided lanyards and they were ready to go.

When Knock had his badge hanging around his neck, Logan smiled. "Perfect. Now all we need to do is figure out how to get off the moon once we rescue Raj and Shayna."

"That might be a little harder." Eddie pulled out a map of the moon installation and spread it out on the table. "I think your best option is to get back on the Lift. Maybe you can activate it with your Level-Five key. It takes an hour to get to the moon and forty minutes to return to Earth. You'll have forty minutes to figure out what to do when you get here. The place will be surrounded with Enforcers by then."

"Can I disable communications between the moon and Earth?" Logan asked.

Eddie scratched his scraggly beard. "I might be able to hack into the system and reroute their communications to me."

"That would be great but would it include internet, texting and all personal phones?"

Eddie shook his head. "Uh, no, but if they thought their messages were getting through in a normal way, why would they augment it with all that other stuff? I think you'd be pretty safe."

Logan sighed. "We'll try to go that route then. What do we do if the Lift is not an option?"

"Space port." Knock pointed to the map. "We can get to a space ship through the service tunnel, commandeer a ship and take off for the stars."

"That's not funny," Logan snarled.

Knock shrugged and smiled. "I wasn't kidding. Anything would be better than coming back here and being sent right back to the moon under guard. You might find that an option, but if I'm jetting into space, I want to do it on my own terms."

"He's right, you know," Eddie said. "Maybe I ought to go with you."

Chapter Eighteen

Logan's smile lasted until they were ready to go. Eddie checked the schedule. The Lift went to the moon twice a day. The next trip was in two hours. The boys had to get there and get into place as soon as possible.

Eddie had decided to go with them, but he chose a different disguise. He was dressed as a technician. He had the uniform and the right badge. Logan narrowed his eyes. "You've done this before."

"Uh, maybe once or twice. Sometimes you have to hardwire. Hacking just ain't enough."

"What part of the Lift will you be in?" Knock asked.

"There's an office and a travel compartment for Company employees. This badge is for a Level Six tech. It should take me all the way to the moon."

Logan slapped Eddie on the back. "We'll have an inside man."

"No, not really. This will get me there. Security on the moon is ridiculous. They'll have a manifest and I won't be on it."

"What will you do?"

Eddie shrugged. "I'll think of something."

"Dude, where will we meet?" Knock asked.

"I'll meet you in the corridor at the construction entrance. If it's not open, I'll try to fix it. I don't have a space suit, so I can't force it. If the construction entrance bombs, we'll meet in the service tunnel under the facility."

Logan's heart raced. This entire plan was filled with crazy risks. "Why are you coming with us again?"

Eddie laughed and followed Logan out the door. "There's no way you guys are leaving me behind. If you end up jetting into space, I want on that ship."

Logan tilted his head and thought. "Is that where we should be aiming anyway? You think heading for the stars is our best bet?"

Eddie shrugged. "It's where I'd want to go if I were you. I'd want to find my father and start a new life. Earth is all about living underground and hiding. Out there, you could start over like the pioneers or the Pilgrims."

Knock picked up his small pack and moved toward the steps leading to the shop overhead. "Eddie, this isn't like something we should leave until the last minute."

"We'll try for the Lift," Logan finally decided. "I don't think I'm ready to be a pioneer. I mean, I'd like to find my dad, but stealing a space ship. That's crazy. At least, it feels like a crazy idea. Am I wrong?"

Eddie shrugged. "Maybe, but Earth is finished, Loge. The future is in the stars. Pretty soon this will be a dead-end planet, a Company stronghold. They'll flush out all the Vagrants and mole people and cover the Earth in concrete. All the food and raw materials will come from out there and life here for anyone not working for the Company will just get harder and harder. At least, that's how I see it. I heard the Vagrants in New LA are building their own spaceship. They got a good organization out there. They're thinking ahead, planning. There's even an organized resistance with plans for taking down the Company."

"You know these people?" Knock said.

Eddie looked away. "I'm in contact."

Logan didn't know what to say to Eddie. His arguments sounded logical, but jetting for the stars was a terrifying thought and one he didn't want to entertain unless it was forced on him. "You could be right. I'm not sayin' you are, but you could be. I just ain't sure I'm ready for it."

Eddie nodded. "I feel you."

"But if after we rescue Raj and Shayna, getting on the Lift looks impossible, it's the space port." He moved close to Knock and whispered. "Can you fly a space ship?"

Knock's startled expression said everything. "Hell no. Hey Eddie can you fly a space ship?"

Eddie grinned. "Won't know until I try. They're mostly computerized and I do know computers."

The three of them went topside. It was very early in the morning. A mist so cold Logan could feel it through his space suit hung close to the ground. The streets were dark and empty of any citizens. Sopore had them all unconscious. The city that never slept was out cold.

They had two hours to get to the Lift, which left at six, and find a way on board. Each carried a chip and Eddie had Shayna's credit disk. He flagged a robo-cab and they climbed inside.

The unmanned cab was warm and dry, the inside sterile and plastic. A Three-D screen mounted on the front showed a steady stream of ads for free everything if you just shipped off world to work in a rapidly growing service industry based around the mines. The cab lifted, the wheels folded under and it shot toward the Lift which was located at the northern-most point of Manhattan in what used to be the Cloisters Museum. The Lift itself was housed in the old bell tower of the reconstructed abbey. The rest of the medieval buildings and the ornamental gardens had been turned into parking lots and support facilities. The once-great landmark built from the parts of four different European abbeys in the nineteen-thirties, no longer existed.

The closer to The Cloisters the cab got, the harder Logan found it to breathe. He was betting his life and that of his friends on this crazy scheme to rescue Raj and Shayna. He'd never done anything like this before. He wasn't used to the responsibility. Vagrants pretty well adopted an every man for themselves attitude. When he ran errands for the Professor, he was usually alone. Raj had only been along to train. Logan was supposed to show him the ropes and he'd lost him. What if Eddie and Knock died as a result of this crazy mission? Logan didn't think he could bear the guilt.

The three of them huddled together on the cab's single bench seat as the vehicle negotiated the streets on a cushion of air. Logan leaned close to Knock and Eddie. "Uh, guys, I can probably do this myself. You don't have to risk your lives if you don't want to."

Eddie held a finger to his lips and pointed to a tiny ear next to the inside light, blinking green. Next to it was the ubiquitous lens of a camera. Logan nodded and sat back against the tough plastic seat. He wasn't feeling very confident. Eddie took a tiny black box the size of a dime with a miniscule antenna out of his pocket and attached it to the camera. A flash lit up the lens and then it went black and Eddie removed his bug. He dug into his small pack and handed Logan a can of computer blast. "Here, this is for any cameras you think might be dangerous."

Logan took it and nodded as he stuffed it into his small pack.

The cab climbed the hill to Fort Tryon Park in Upper Manhattan. It went through the old wrought-iron gates and climbed the boulevard to the ancient castle on top of the hill. When the cab pulled right under the rock-faced porte-cochere of The Cloisters,

Logan leaned forward and gave the auto-pilot new directions. "Please pull around to the service entrance."

This was no place for them to exit. Arched doorways from some abbey in Europe opened up to the main lobby of the Lift. The whole place had been retrofitted to accommodate a bunch of tourists wanting to visit the moon. Busses were parked all along the circular drive leading to the front entrance. Tourists were everywhere milling around as they waited for their tour guides to lead them to the Lift and an adventure. They walked slowly and seemed very complacent and happy thanks to Sopore. The front door was definitely not where Logan wanted to get out of this cab.

The cab doors slid shut and the hover car moved slowly around the rock wall on a narrow track. It finally stopped at high green gates clearly marked "Service Entrance."

When the doors opened, they scrambled out and plastered themselves against the rock wall. "Okay, Mastermind," Eddie whispered. "What now?"

"You're wearing the tech suit. Ring the bell."

Before Eddie could so much as touch the buzzer, the gate slid open and a garbage truck inched through. Logan, Knock and Eddie ran for the trees where they crouched and watched the truck roll down the track their cab had just come in on. Logan checked his watch. "Forty-two minutes until the Lift takes off."

Eddie patted Logan on the back. "Stop worrying. We'll make it."

When the truck was gone, they ran back to the gate. Eddie looked around, leaned over and pressed a red button inside a glass box. Deep inside the building a buzzer sounded. A disembodied voice came through the box. "State your business."

Eddie picked up his badge and held it to the view screen. "Donny Ling; I'm here to fix the data access for the magnetic drum heads moon side. They got a glitch in the system and I'm the only one who knows how to fix it."

Logan lifted an eyebrow and Eddie shrugged.

"I don't have a notation here about any glitch or any Donny Ling scheduled for the moon."

Eddie shoved his oriental face close to the camera feed. Four more cameras hummed into action and focused on him. "Listen, dork, I got the call. If you don't wanna let me in and the Lift crashes on its return trip because you don't have a notation, I'm not taking the fall. I showed up. Make a freaking notation of that!"

Logan heard a click and the gates began whining open. Eddie smiled. "Thank you."

Eddie stalked in like he owned the place. When the gates began to close, Logan took out Eddie's can of computer blast and sprayed the view screen and the lenses of the four cameras. With all of them covered in an icy fog, they waited until the gate was almost shut and slipped through.

They now had forty minutes to get into the nose compartment of the Lift. Eddie headed straight for the docking area while Logan and Knock lagged behind. Logan led Knock to a secluded corner of The Cloisters that used to be part of the ornamental gardens. He hunkered down behind a stone bench, pulled out a map of the facility and pointed to two access corridors for loading baggage and freight. Knock nodded and they moved through a maze of dark hallways lined with the stones from four different European abbeys. They didn't see any of the tourists or Lift personnel. These tunnels must rarely be used. The stone walls and floors made it cold and dark. Overhead, yellow lights inside tiny metal cages cast an eerie glow over the flagstones and walls. Logan imagined this was what it was like to live back in Medieval times. A tunnel just like this may have led to a dungeon, a burial catacomb or even an oubliette.

In front of them, Logan heard activity. They stopped at the exit. The huge Lift capsule sat in the open tower surrounded by enormous gray metal boxes with slotted vents in rows on each side. Thick coils of wire and conduit snaked out of the boxes and into a bank of transformers. The Lift reached from the basement all the way to the top of the stone tower. Ten stories above them was the glass nose. A train of freight was being loaded into the lower compartments. Logan and Knock strolled casually by workers wearing the glassy stare of people stoned on Sopore. Hunched over, lost in their little drugged-out world, they loaded boxes and pallets of goods into the capsule with a propane-powered fork lift. Logan could smell the fumes. These guys weren't destined to live long.

A senior longshoreman looked up and noticed Knock. He smiled, stopped manipulating a robotic arm, and walked over to them. Logan's heart began to pound. "Agent Fargo," the man said as he eyed Knock's chest appreciatively. "Remember me? I met you when they opened the new wing here."

Knock's eyes ratcheted around inside the female agent's mask like blue marbles. Logan gave a tiny shrug. The worker had a badge that said Ralph Munching, lead load technician. "Ralph," Knock said in a high falsetto. "Of course I remember you. You were, uh, drinking champagne?"

"No, that was Amos. I was playing piano."

Knock nodded. "Of course, how could I forget?"

"Hey, listen, if you ever get time, would you like to go for coffee? I know a great place close to Riverbank Park. The view of the Hudson is amazing."

Knock tittered and Logan's stomach rolled. This was taking so much time. He glanced at his com watch and saw they only had twelve minutes left. The longshoremen were closing the baggage hatches preparing for takeoff.

"We should be running," he said to Knock in a voice that squeaked.

Ralph looked at him funny and Logan did the only thing he could. He bopped him across the back of his skull with the can of computer blast. The guy dropped into Knock's waiting arms.

"We're almost out of time. We have to move," Logan gasped. "What do we do with him? He'll alert security sure as heck."

"Kill him?"

Logan shook his head. "I couldn't."

They ended up shoving him into the well around the base of the Lift. He dropped the fifteen feet to the bottom and didn't move. With Ralph out of the way, they ran to the scaffolding erected for servicing the outside of the Lift. Knock scrambled up the ladder first followed by Logan whose nerves were zinging. He could feel the hair on his neck crawling and he fought the urge to round his shoulders. They scampered up the ladder to the nose. A small access door was closed. Logan took his Level-Five key out and plugged it in the circular lock. He turned it and the panel opened. Knock crawled through and Logan, after glancing once over his shoulder, followed him. He looked at his watch. Five minutes to get up to the nose and buckle in.

When the door was shut behind him, they crawled as fast as they could down the tubular access. It was lit with blue strips in the ceiling. The tube ended at another door requiring the key. This opened to a vertical tube with a ladder set into the wall; down led to the passenger compartment, up led to the nose.

"Hurry," Logan moaned. "We're never gonna make it."

He raced up the ladder to another locked door and glanced down at Knock hanging onto the ladder below him. Without Hump's key they would never have gotten anywhere near the moon, at least not on the Lift. He held his finger to his lips and pointed to the tiniest ear he'd ever seen blinking red above his head. Knock nodded.

Logan pulled himself through the circular opening at the top of the tube and scooted out of the way so Knock could climb inside. With the door locked behind them, Logan quickly examined the space. Eddie had checked the manifest. The two seats designed for joyriders searching for a thrill unavailable anywhere else on Earth, were rarely booked. They cost a fortune. These seats were Logan's destination.

The roof of the Lift's nose was made of layers of a clear plastic polymer so hard nothing could break it. Two cushioned blast chairs were set into a depression. The rest of the space was filled with electrical boxes, flat computer modems and wires. Logan prayed nothing up here did need servicing.

He and Knock crawled to the chairs and dropped into them as a low whine began to build under them. "Strap in," he ordered Knock. "Time is almost up." He pointed to his comm.

When they were strapped in and the whine had increased to a roar, he risked sending a message to Eddie. He was worried about his friend. He and Knock were safe for the moment.

The roar increased and the Lift started vibrating as a message clicked into his watch. He glanced at it as his heart raced with excitement. No matter what happened, this was going to be the ride of a lifetime. He shoved his wrist in front of Knock who nodded. Eddie was strapped in in the technicians' cabin waiting for takeoff.

Over their heads a blinding tube of light shot out from under the capsule and straight into the early-dawn sky in an unbroken line to the full moon high above. Logan reached out and flipped Knock's face-plate down, closed his own and then grabbed the armrests. Riding in the nose must be like riding in the front seats of the scariest rollercoaster made. This was going to be a hair-raising experience.

The whining grew into a crescendo. The capsule vibrated as the rays of the rising sun turned the Hudson River a brilliant gold. Logan took a breath. He almost closed his eyes, but thought, this was probably going to be something he better watch.

The vibrations increased and the whining grew into a physical presence. Logan felt it in his teeth. Suddenly, the Lift shot up the magnetic column over their heads traveling at an unimaginable speed. Logan's face was pulled back, his mask slipped and he grabbed it before it covered his eyes. Holding it in place, he watched in horrified fascination as the capsule streaked toward the moon. He wanted to scream but didn't have enough breath. Next to him Knock's shriek disappeared into the thunderous roar swirling around them.

Chapter Nineteen

"Whoa," Logan whispered when the Lift finally stopped. "What a rush."

Logan breathed out a long sigh of relief. It was over and they were on the moon. That was the good news. The bad news was now they had to figure out how to get out of the capsule.

Knock groaned. "I think I crapped in my pants."

Logan pointed to his mask. "I don't think our fake identities are going to work anymore." The blast through ten thousand miles of Earth's atmosphere had pushed both of their synthetic cheeks into a gigantic smile.

Knock ripped his off and Logan followed suit. Logan sniffed. "I think we have air, but don't count on it lasting. Button up your suit." He dropped his face plate and fastened it tightly. Knock did the same.

Logan unsnapped his crash harness and slowly began floating up. "No gravity," he said to Knock. "Look, Ma, I can fly."

"What do we do about getting out of this thing?" Knock said into his ear bud. "I don't think popping out in the debarking area is gonna work for us now."

Logan examined their small pod. It mostly consisted of the giant clear dome over their heads. Knock pointed at what appeared to be a small escape hatch set into the wall for emergency purposes. "How about that?"

The hatch was round and locked with a red bar that read for emergency use only. Logan nodded. "That looks like our best bet if we want to get around the guards. And as far as I'm concerned, this qualifies as an emergency."

"And just where do you think it's going to come out?" Knock said as he flicked his fingers in an attempt to remove long strands of rubbery glue from the mask that had adhered to his space suit gloves. "This crap is like permanent."

"Quit foolin' around," Logan snarled. "We're on the moon for crying out loud. We could be dragged out of here at any minute."

When Logan stood up, he immediately felt blood rush to his head. The lack of gravity in this part of the capsule had him dizzy and disoriented. He floated to the roof and bumped against the clear polymer. He quickly discovered he wasn't the first person to realize there was no gravity up here, and grabbed a handle set into the wall for just such a purpose. He stared in fascination through the glass of the roof. On one side, the outside world looked to be an ocean of white. On the other, a tall block building rose high above the Lift.

"I think that hatch leads to the surface."

After clamping his face plate firmly in place, he crawled down the side of the roof to the escape hatch using the handholds.

Knock was still pressed against the clear polymer of the roof trying to follow him. "I think I'm gonna hurl," he moaned.

Logan pressed his com button so he could talk directly into Knock's suit. "You better not. Come on, Knock, get down here. We gotta go."

Knock finally figured out how to use the handholds. He hung upside down beside Logan, grinning. "Once you get over the urge to blow chunks, this is way cool."

Logan slowly and carefully pushed the bar down to open the hatch. When the door opened, he breathed a sigh of relief. "Good thing we wore these suits. This part of the capsule isn't pressurized

VAGRANT

any more. Down there," he pointed below where the passengers rode. "They have pressure or they'd all need suits."

"Let's do some moon walking," Knock said. "Where's the map? We need to know which way to go."

Logan felt a rush of hope. Maybe they *were* going to rescue Raj and Shayna. Maybe this would work after all. "The map is in my head, dude. I memorized it. I'm gonna go first. I guess that makes you Buzz Aldrin, and I'm Astronaut Neil Armstrong."

Logan shoved his head through the hatch. It was a tight squeeze. He finally wiggled through and paused to hang onto the hatch. "There's enough gravity to pull my feet down," he told Knock. "I'm gonna try a jump."

He launched himself off the side of the Lift and flew across the rough lunar landscape. He shouldn't have thrust so hard. He finally descended, falling end over end. The struggle to gain his feet caused him to land on his head. He bounced once, then righted himself. The view froze him in place and he gasped as he caught sight of Earth. It was the most beautiful thing he'd ever seen. No words could describe the sheer majesty of it. "Dude," was all he could think of to say.

He was still staring when Knock crashed into him. They tumbled out of control higher and higher until Logan figured out he had a grav button in the control panel set into the arm of his suit. He punched it, with his heart leaping out of his chest. All he could think of was this was the wrong way, and a bad time to go back to Earth.

The grav button activated his gravity boots. Slowly, his feet dropped beneath him. He held onto Knock, pointed to the button on Knock's suit and slowly descended. When his feet touched the rocky soil, he almost kissed the ground.

An alarm bell suddenly clanged loud enough to reach Logan inside his suit. "I think we're screwed," he said to Knock.

"What do we do?" Knock moaned.

Logan examined the control panel. "We've got jets. Use 'em." He pushed the button on his arm and felt the jets ignite. "Let's pray we have tons of fuel."

"This is a Wal-Mart suit," Knock snapped. "We'll be lucky to get a minute of lift time."

Logan knew from the map where the construction entrance of the prison was located. Unfortunately, it was on the other side of the prison from where they now were. When he glanced back at the Lift, he shouted a warning to Knock. "We got company."

Two moon buggies, outfitted with ridiculously large balloon tires, shot out of an open door and after them. Inside the cab of each one was an enforcer. On the moon, they didn't wear black suits and ties, but their space suits were black with red lettering. Logan could read SS from where he stood frozen with fear.

"Let's jam!" Knock shouted and slapped Logan. The blow shot Logan out of his moment of terror and about twenty feet. He turned his jets and shot around the side of the prison.

The two of them jetted a lot faster than the buggies could travel across the rocky moon surface. When the buggies had to dodge a boulder, the two boys went over. They were gaining ground when a red alarm began beeping on Logan's instrument panel. "I think we're running out of fuel."

"What do we do?"

"Bounce?" Logan turned off his jets to save the rest of his fuel and began leaping forward so he could cover more ground like he was a giant kangaroo. Knock followed suit and soon the two of them were bouncing across the surface of the moon laughing like maniacs. "This is a blast!" Knock yelled.

Logan glanced behind and saw the buggies were losing more ground, but they refused to go away. When he and Knock closed in on a corner of the prison, Logan knew after one more corner, the construction entrance would appear as an old makeshift roof covering a faint track which led into the building. But when they rounded the corner, two more moon buggies sped toward them. They were trapped!

Logan hit his jets and pointed. "Up!" he said and turned the jets straight so he went up the wall of the prison. The building was only two stories here, just a long, low, flat building. He reached the roof, which had to repel meteors but not rain so it was the same material as the walls, concrete block. They stopped and looked over the building's edge at the four buggies just pulling up to the wall. The Enforcers got out and without pausing hit their jets, shooting toward them as they continued the chase without a pause.

"Crap!" Logan snarled. "Run."

Chapter Twenty

Shayna's new quarters were in the isolation pod. She was locked in a cell in a row of them filled with female criminals the Company had decided could be rehabilitated by working in the mines. She missed her new friends and worried about poor Cressy with no mother and no one to look out for her.

As she lay on her cot and stared at the ceiling, she contemplated the hopelessness of her situation. Buried inside the prison, the only way of marking time was the twenty-four hour clock on the wall. According to it, it was eight in the morning on the East Coast of Earth. Far down the row she heard a scream. She ran to the bars and looked down the alley toward the screaming.

Raj realized who the woman who had tried to talk to him was about an hour after he went back to the men's pod and lay on his cot. He'd been trying to avoid eating Sopore infused food, but it was really hard in the detention center. His thought processes were slower and he had issues with motivation, as in he wasn't. Sopore made you not question anything. You happily accepted the most bizarre stuff. You didn't give a rat's behind about anything. So he had to fight it.

The woman who accosted him in the dish room was the Candy Striper he met with Logan by the Dumpster's at the hospital. Somehow she must have hooked up with Logan. She had a message from him. The thought bounced around his brain all night. When he was rousted to go on duty in the kitchen at seven-thirty in the morning, he took a back way through the shower rooms into the women's section. He figured they had her in a cell as a troublemaker so he slipped into the cell block slightly before eight.

The cells were locked but Raj wasn't worried. He was the official janitor for the cells in the men's detention center so he was in the system. He stepped in front of a plate just inside the access door and pressed his face against it. A facial recognition scanner ran down the plate. He heard the metallic click indicating the cells were open and began walking down the center alley.

He was halfway down the row, examining each one, when one of the guards opened the access door and started toward him. His only option was to dive into a cell.

He shot into the first one he saw. A large woman lay sprawled across her cot snoring loudly, the thin legs of the bed bending beneath her weight. He rolled under it to hide from the guard and hit one of the legs. The strained structure gave out and collapsed, dropping the woman two feet onto Raj. The woman continued to snore. Sopore induced sleep was deep and heavy.

Raj squirmed beneath the woman's weight. She was too heavy. He couldn't breathe, but suffered in silence until the guard walked all the way down the alley and exited into the main pod; then he grunted and threw her off. That's when she woke up. She screamed and kept on screaming. Raj rolled out from under the crushed cot and looked up. Temporarily blinded by the sight of a massive pair of legs and lady parts, he stumbled out of the cell and into the next one as the guard, hearing the commotion, reentered the high-security area.

The woman in his new haven grabbed him and stuffed him under her blanket. "Hide here," she whispered.

Her neighbor was till screaming when the guard barged in demanding to know what was going on. The frightened woman could only manage monosyllabic answers which explained nothing. The guard told her to pipe down, slammed her door and stalked back down the alley, exiting to the main pod.

"Who are you?" The woman who'd stuffed him under her blankets whispered. She lifted a corner and smiled. "Oh my, you are adorable."

Out of the frying pan into the fire. "Hi, I am Raj. I'm here to find my friend."

Shayna spotted Raj after the guard left. She'd heard the locks on the doors click and knew they were open. Raj was here and this would likely be her only opportunity to speak to him. She pushed her door open slowly, looked up and down the alley, and ran to rescue him from the attentions of the cell's inmate. After one more look up and down the alley, she flung open the door and grabbed his arm. "Hurry, I have to talk to you before you're discovered."

"No, wait, I found him first," the owner of the cell protested and grabbed Raj's arm.

Shayna put a hand on her arm. "I know, but he's only a boy and he came here to see me. It's really important for all of us."

The woman dropped onto her cot. "S'not fair. No one comes to see me."

Raj turned and bowed to her. "Thank you most sincerely for rescuing me from . . . from the guard."

Shayna pulled him into her cell, but left her door ajar. She had no faith in these Company employees. They could decide to check the locks at any time. "Raj, I'm so glad to see you. How did you find me?"

Raj's dark skin turned the color of purple grapes. "I, uh, knew they'd put you here. I've been here long enough to know how these things work, you see."

She pulled him into a hug. He squirmed and she let him go. "I was sure I'd never find you. This is amazing. You sound just like the Professor, by the way."

"He is my uncle."

As they sat on her cot, she poured out her story. "I think Logan is coming to rescue you. He booked passage on one of the Tong ships to the moon."

Raj shook his head. "That is very bad. The Tong is working hand in glove with the Company. They pretend to be outlaws but the Company knows everything they do. I heard they have branched out to other planets and have established space ports on Exxon and Gliese."

Shayna's heart rose into her throat and she covered her mouth with her hand. "Oh, no. But he paid them for a berth. They'll bring him here, won't they?"

Raj shrugged. "I'll keep alert in case he tries to contact me and we must pray it is so, but you never know. They are not to be trusted."

He was just rising to leave when the alarms sounded and the cell doors up and down the row locked with a noisy metallic clunk.

Raj looked at her and she looked at him. "Logan!" They said together.

Raj grabbed her hand. "Come with me. You can't be locked in here."

He dragged her into the alley and they ran to an access door at the end. He pulled her through as the door made a noise and the lock engaged.

****

Logan and Knock raced across the roof, covering huge distances by leaping. The Enforcers behind them knew the tactic and pursued with determination. Logan didn't know where he was. He'd lost his sense of direction the minute they hit the roof. He spotted an opening up ahead and pointed it out to Knock as he keyed his com unit. "Looks like an air vent."

"No!" Knock said. "We'll die."

"We're not doing too good now, buddy. That vent looks like our only chance."

"It's too dangerous, Loge. Stop."

Logan hopped over a huge dome of the clear polymer with Knock chasing him. The clear dome must be some kind of viewing station for tourists or guards. Logan had seen several. When they got to the air vent, he leaned over and stared down into the long tube. Below, huge fans turned slowly sucking used air out of the building and expelling it into the empty atmosphere. Logan tried to figure a way through the fans and finally got an idea. "The fans will eat us if we just drop. I'm gonna jet into them."

Knock grabbed his arm. "No way. Don't Loge. You'll die, man."

Logan shook him off. "Gotta. Only way."

"You can't. It's too risky."

Logan saw the Enforcers leaping toward them across the roof. "I gotta try."

He tapped out a message for Eddie giving him the best guess he had for their location. From what he remembered of his Dad's three-D map he was somewhere above the detention center for women being transported off world. But it was just a guess. "Here goes nothing," he whispered over the comm.

"Logan." Knock reached his gloved hand out to stop him but Logan had already hit his jets. He prayed he had enough fuel leftover to make it as he shot head first into the vent, tucked his arms to his side and used his head like a ram. The suit's helmet collided with the fan blade which had not been designed to handle much stress. It bent and impacted another blade. Logan got tossed for a moment as the fan skewed sideways and dropped to the bottom of the shaft with Logan shooting after it. He turned off the jets and shook his head as he slowly sank to the bottom. The blade lay in pieces across a bed of gravel.

Knock slowly descended into the air shaft while Logan shook off the effects of a slight concussion. "That musta hurt," Knock said as he opened an access door and shoved Logan toward it.

"Not as much as I thought it would."

"I gotta say, you're fan-tastic." Knock grinned.

"Not funny."

They scrambled into the service tunnel and started crawling. The tunnel exited inside a huge room filled with oxygen-manufacturing equipment, air scrubbers, blowers and conditioners. The noise was deafening.

Logan didn't slow down. He ran across the room to an airlock and hit the button to open it. The automatic door slicked open and they shot into the waiting chamber. When the door to the air plant was closed behind them, he opened the exit door and they raced out. Logan stopped halfway down the service tunnel and went back. He opened the door to the airlock and looked around. "I wanna jam this inner door open. If it won't close, the outer door to the air plant won't open."

Knock grinned. "I got this." He grabbed a huge fire extinguisher off the wall, smashed the door repeatedly until it was too dented to make a seal, then lodged it in the door. The automatic door tried to close, hit the giant red canister and stopped.

"It should slow the Enforcers down."

Logan ran down the tunnel. "Yeah, but the facility knows we're here. We gotta work fast or we're screwed. I need to know where we are. Let's find a place where I can open the GPS map Eddie keyed into my helmet."

Knock stopped, walked back to a door and pushed it open. Logan peered inside. A small room was filled with space suits. There were some old ones, big bulky things suitable for work on the space station, and many of the lighter suits like he and Knock wore which had been specifically created for work on the moon. Knock followed him in and Logan keyed the GPS.

On the inside of his helmet, a map of the prison appeared with their location a beeping red dot. Only Logan could see it. "We're in a service tunnel under the women's detention area," he said to Knock. "Remember the service tunnels Eddie told us about? This tube we're in goes to that main junction and then there's a huge open service area for equipment and storage for supplies. There's a disposal system for garbage which includes an incinerator."

"Gotta love an incinerator. But shouldn't we try to get up and into the women's pod? I mean if we're under it."

Logan tapped his faceplate. "According to this map, there's no way up there from this tunnel. We have to get to the hub."

"What're you gonna tell Eddie?"

"To meet us inside the incinerator . . . unless it's on." He grinned. Logan tapped this info out on the com unit hoping Eddie could find them. "The planned meeting site of the construction entrance is obviously not gonna work anymore."

"If we can't get to the women's pod from here, how're we gonna find Raj and Shayna?" Knocked asked.

"I'm thinking."

Knock punched his arm. "I shoulda known. I can see smoke coming from your helmet."

The walk down the tube to the central service depot took twenty minutes. They got lost once down a dead-end tunnel and had to key the GPS again. By the time they arrived at their destination, they were both exhausted and running on empty.

"We need food, dude, and some rest," Knock said as they closed in on the hub.

"Can't until we're somewhere safe. And this ain't safe."

Up ahead, lights illuminated a huge open area. As they neared it they slowed to reconnoiter. Logan stopped at the tunnel's exit and stared at the busy service center. Workers in space suits hustled low boys filled with crates and boxes. Robots manned by a rider moved pallets of goods from one spot to another. A small train pulled by a robot engine was filled with more crates. The train shot away from them down a large tunnel leading into the main part of the facility.

"Holy crap!" Knock whispered. "What do we do now?"

Logan pointed to a lighted office in the center of the hub. It was filled with people in space suits with their helmets off. "That's the office." He pointed off to the left. "Back there is storage for everything. Behind the storage are the garbage chute and the incinerator."

"How do we get there through all this?"

Logan shrugged. "We try to look like we belong. Grab a box."

When they stepped into the open, Logan felt unbelievably exposed. As they moved into the center of all the activity, he saw pairs of Enforcers in their black suits walking slowly, examining everyone. They carried blasters across their forearms ready to shoot. Logan had never lived a safe kind of life, but this was the most dangerous situation he'd ever imagined. He swallowed hard and kept on walking.

When Knock crowded too close, Logan elbowed him. "Get off me, man. You look like you're ready to freak out. Chill and try to look a little less guilty."

They edged toward the storage area carrying their boxes. Logan's was heavy, but he wasn't about to complain or put it down. He held it in front of his face as they skirted a robotic forklift and one of the robots with a driver, its huge mechanical arms carrying a giant drum of some kind of liquid.

A sign pointed the way to the garbage chute. Another train scooted past them loaded with trash containers overflowing with garbage. They fell in behind it, walking at a fast pace. So far, no one had noticed them.

Chapter Twenty-One

Shayna and Raj emerged from the women's detention center and disappeared into the vast kitchens. Raj had no idea what to do with her. The kitchen was mostly manned by men, but there were some women. Hiding her here seemed like the only plan available. On the wall, red alarms blinked. The facility was on high alert. Everything would be locked down, but the detainees still had to eat.

He took Shayna's hand and led her to banks of walk-in coolers. On hooks outside each cooler were rubber aprons. He leaned close to her. All around them pots clanged, people murmured in the low, slow voice of the Sopore addicted, and the smell of food cooking swirled. "Take this and put it on." He handed her an apron. "See these coolers. If we get separated or anyone stops you or asks anything hide in number-three."

Shayna's big brown eyes were wide with fear. She nodded. "Okay."

"Follow me," he told her as he wove his way between massive stove tops manned by cooks wearing white aprons. "Keep your head down."

He took her to his world, the dish area. Once there, he led her to the rear where vast sinks filled with hot water and dirty pots and pans awaited. "Start washing."

Raj glanced around. Nothing looked out of the ordinary. He started washing the dirty pots. When he glanced up, he jumped. Two Enforcers wearing space suits were headed toward them. Each carried a nasty-looking black blaster resting across their arms. The dish room was filled with bad odors, dirty dishes, giant trash containers of reeking garbage, steam from hot soapy water and the clatter of the monstrous mechanized dish washer. Raj guessed it didn't look inviting. The Enforcers eyed each person in the back of the room for a moment, then walked on. Shayna rolled her eyes and sighed loud enough for him to hear. They both continued to wash dishes, but Raj's attention was on the door of the dish room. He wasn't surprised when the Enforcers came back. One of them held a scanner and Raj gasped. The enforcer was searching for chips.

When he pointed it at Shayna, Raj heard the beep and knew she'd been made. He shoved her toward the walk-in coolers. "Run!"

She stumbled on the two-inch thick rubber mat right behind her foot and went down on one knee. The enforcer grabbed her and whipped out a set of plasti-cuffs. "Hold it Shayna Nagata. You're supposed to be in the women's detention center."

He turned to his partner. "This is the one we're looking for. She's slated to be shipped off tomorrow on the small transport to Exxon."

The partner dropped his weapon to look at the screen on the scanner and that's when Raj whacked him in the head with an enormous frying pan. The pan was filled with water as well. It doused the enforcer with a flood of filthy dishwater. His partner dropped Shayna and the scanner to help him and she bolted. Raj didn't hesitate. He caught the second enforcer on his backswing using all his strength to smash him in the head with the bottom of the pan. The blow laid the tall enforcer out cold on his back in the inch of gray water covering the dish room floor.

Terror filled Raj and he was slow to react, probably because of Sopore, and the enforcer he'd smacked first grabbed a handful of his gray one-piece jumpsuit. Raj climbed into the sinks, shucked his jumpsuit, leaped out spraying sanitized water everywhere, and pounded after Shayna wearing only his gray boxers and his boots as he prayed to his uncle's gods that she'd gone to the walk-in as planned.

The enforcer he'd hit first tried to follow, but Raj's fellow workers suddenly became very stupid and obstructive, stumbling into the enforcer's path, falling in front of him and shoving barrels, crates and sacks of food in his way as they fell. Raj made it down the hallway behind the kitchen, ducked through the door to the prep area and dived into walk-in number-three slamming the door behind him.

Shayna was there shaking with cold in her wet jumpsuit. He grabbed her hand. "Come on. We can't stay here."

She let him tow her out of the walk-in. A commotion in the kitchen alerted him to the arrival of more Enforcers. A train of trash barrels was just leaving through the big double doors in the back. He pulled Shayna to the train, moving slowly into the access tunnel. She understood what he planned. They jumped onto the last trailer together and Raj lifted the lid of one of the barrels. "Get in."

Shayna balked. The odor from the bin was really bad. Raj pleaded. "You have to. It's our only hope of getting out of here."

Holding her nose, she rolled her eyes as she scrambled into the bin. "There's no room."

"Throw some trash out. No one will notice."

She heaved armfuls of reeking garbage onto the trailer bed, finally fit herself in, and Raj slammed the lid. He found one for himself, squeezed inside, stomping garbage down under his feet and body until he could close the lid. Huddled inside the stinking container, he felt the train picking up speed as it headed down the ramp to the service tunnels.

Logan and Knock leaned against the wall of the noisy garbage sorter and munched apples they'd filched from a bag of spoiled ones thrown into the trash. The garbage from the prison would take care of a Vagrant colony for a year. They were unbelievably wasteful.

"Did you see anything else in there we can eat?" Knock asked around a mouthful of apple.

"There's at least ten loaves of bread, but I'm sure it's full of Sopore."

Knock sighed. "Eating a little wouldn't hurt."

Logan socked him in the shoulder. "You're kidding. We need to stay alert, not stumble around like Sopore goons."

Knock pouted. "I can't be alert when I'm starving!"

Logan hushed him. "Keep your voice down. I hear another train coming."

One of the robot trains turned down the wide alley leading to the sorting center. It pulled in and docked its three trailers at the unloading platform. The trailers started to tilt, lids automatically opened, and garbage flowed out of the containers onto a moving belt. Logan noticed this was another load from the kitchens and walked over to see if there was anything he and Knock could eat. He saw two cucumbers, was reaching out to get them when the next container in line, tilted, opened up and dumped Shayna on top of him.

He didn't recognize her at first. She was covered with dripping garbage and wore a shapeless one-piece gray suit. She groaned and reached for his hand. "Help me."

Without thinking, he grabbed her under the arms which transferred a lot of her garbage to him. He put her on the floor, was scraping spoiled lettuce and partially eaten food off his space suit, when Raj tumbled out of the next container. He recognized his friend right away. "Raj!"

"Help Shayna, will you?" Raj jumped up and started cleaning cottage cheese and soy burger off his almost-naked body.

Knock grabbed Raj and hugged him while Logan bent to help Shayna up. "Dude, where're your clothes?"

Logan picked Shayna up and held her out in front of him for an entire minute. Her eyes lit with warmth when she realized it was him and she threw herself into his arms. "Logan, you made it!"

He held her close enjoying the feel of her in his arms even though she smelled awful and he was wearing a space suit. She pulled his head down and kissed him. He responded for a few seconds. This was only their second real kiss. But time was not on their side. The sound of running feet grew steadily louder. The SS!

"They must have figured out where we went," Raj said.

Logan set Shayna aside and ran to the door. He looked down the wide alley leading to the hub and saw the first black suit round the corner. "We gotta get out of here."

"Where do we go?" Knock glanced around the room frantically.

Logan dropped his face plate and pulled up the map. He zoomed in and saw there was no escape route that didn't go through the sorter which led to the compacter. He noted the alley just outside the door led to a service tunnel and the spaceport. "We have to go out."

"But there're Enforcers out there," Raj said.

"Can't help it." Logan looked out and around the corner and saw the herd of Enforcers closing in. "Now!" He yelled and shot into the alley.

181

Raj and Shayna erupted from the room followed by Knock holding up the rear. They took off away from the Enforcers and it didn't take Logan long to realize they couldn't outrun them; a conviction that strengthened as soon as the Enforcers opened fire. Blaster shots burned into the block walls exploding a shower of concrete pieces around them.

"They're getting closer," Knock screamed. "Where the hell is Eddie?"

Logan spotted a small hatch in the wall and ran for it, passing Shayna and Raj. He ripped it open. It led to a tunnel. "In here," he beckoned to Shayna. "Hurry!"

"You don't have to tell me that," she snapped as she dove into the tunnel and scrambled forward.

Raj followed, then Knock. A blaster charge hit the door, knocking it off its hinge as Logan shot into the tunnel and started crawling as fast as he could. He heard a scream up ahead that faded and then a splash. Water?

Raj yelled and Knock stopped in front of him. It was dark as a tomb in the tunnel and it smelled awful. "What's wrong?" Logan asked.

"The tunnel ends." Knock crawled forward another inch and used the light on his helmet to illuminate what was in front of him. "Oh no."

"Don't care," Logan mumbled. "Move." He shoved Knock who scrabbled for a moment and then tumbled into the abyss. Logan moved forward, lit his light and stared at the scene in front of him. The smell rising off the garbage in the pit in front of him was worse than the city sewer on a hot day. He glanced behind and saw lights. The Enforcers were thinking about following them into the tunnel but as yet hadn't. There was only one way to go. He dropped into the stinking morass and landed in two feet of liquid. "What is this place?"

"You're the one with the map," Knock snarled. "You figure it out."

Shayna slogged through the mess to cling to his arm as Logan keyed the GPS. What it told him was terrifying. "We're in the compactor," he whispered. "No wonder the Enforcers won't follow us."

"You better contact Eddie and tell him to get us out of here," Knock said.

"I think the compactor just came on," Raj whispered. "Listen."

The hum of machinery grew louder and louder until it was a roar. Terrified, Logan frantically sent a message to Eddie who hadn't answered the last one. He held his breath partially from terror and partially because of the stench. When a vibration on his wrist indicated Eddie had answered, he was almost afraid to look. Eddie was their only hope of getting out of here. Shayna screamed when the floor jolted into life.

"Eddie is looking for a way to turn off the compactor," Logan yelled over the noise.

Eddie had received Logan's message telling him where they should meet, but he was having his own problems. His badge and uniform had ushered him through security and into the facility, but when Logan and Knock were spotted by the SS, and the alert went out, he was detained by a pair of Enforcers on his way to the lower levels. Finally satisfied with his disjointed explanation for why he was in the elevator going down the two Enforcers left him to go up and Eddie had continued, but he'd had to constantly dodge roving pairs of SS and guards. It had taken him a long time to make it to the service level.

When he got the emergency text from Logan, he was in an access tunnel leading to the service hub and the spaceport. He frantically searched for a computer port, found a small console built into the wall beside a bank of elevators, and opened it with a screwdriver. The keyboard was tiny and on a swivel. He moved it out and hacked into the system conscious of the need for speed.

The compactor slowly ground into gear and the floor began carrying everything toward the front of the compartment making chugging sounds. Disgusting water sloshed higher as the floor moved. Shayna whimpered with fear as she clung to Logan who tapped out a frantic note to Eddie to hurry. Knock and Raj climbed over piles of trash to get further away from the front and Logan dragged Shayna after them. When they were leaning against the rear wall, he sent another frantic message to Eddie. They only had ten feet of slowly disappearing space.

Eddie didn't answer and Logan prayed it was because he was busy stopping the compactor. The trash was building in a mound in front of them. Crushing sounds and small explosions only increased their terror. The water kept sloshing but the level was lower. As the room shrunk to eight feet, then six, they climbed higher. They were screwed.

When there was only five feet of space, garbage had risen to the roof. The room they were in apparently fed the compactor, funneling mashed trash into the crusher. Logan kept pulling Shayna higher, clearing space as he went. The ceiling, once twenty feet above them, was now within touching distance. Logan spotted a port in the roof and pointed. "Try to reach it."

Knock scrambled higher, climbing on top of an empty crate and six black bags of trash, grabbed the port and searched it. "No handle on this side," he moaned.

The crushing noises increased and Shayna started crying. "We're gonna die."

The room had shrunk to a mere two feet of space. Garbage threatened to smother them. Logan couldn't feel his feet any longer and was too scared to move. What an ignominious way to go, squashed in garbage, funneled into a compactor and turned into cubed trash.

Raj grabbed his hand. Knock took Raj's hand and Shayna's. Logan held onto Shayna. Linked, they waited for death as the compactor crushed another three inches of garbage and funneled it into the compactor. When they were lying on top of the trash inches from the ceiling, Logan spotted a sliver of space between the compactor and the roof. Whoever designed and built the trash facility had left room to remove the compactor if they so desired and replace it. A metal lip around the compactor's edge funneled the trash down into the compactor and away from the space. Was it big enough for them to fit into?

"Knock, look!" Logan pointed to the open space. Knock nodded and clambered over three bags to get closer. He stuffed his head into the space. It was hard to get into it because of the lip. "I think we can fit." He pushed on the metal lip and got it to give him another two inches. "It looks like it might lead to the other side where the incinerator is."

"Send Raj," Logan snapped as he shoved Raj forward. "Hurry."

Raj took Knock's hand, got dragged across the trash where Knock shoved him into the space. Raj had to crawl like a worm, but was soon gone.

"Shayna, go." Knock tossed her into the space. She had to flatten, but fit.

"You go next," Logan said to Knock.

Knock shook his head. "Not enough time. The compactor had them pressed to within three inches of the wall. "We go together."

Logan nodded and rolled over the lip into the space. He immediately banged his head on the concrete ceiling and had to turn it sideways. His butt hit the ceiling, but he was out of the compactor. Knock pushed in beside him. Beneath them they could feel the garbage being crushed. The metal of the huge compactor was hot. Logan turned his head and saw the wall they'd been leaning against hit the compactor wall and the chugging sound died. All the garbage had either been funneled into the compactor or was smashed between the wall and the machine.

Because they were both in the restricted space it took longer to get to the other side of the huge machine. When Logan's head reached the opening on the other side, he groaned. The fiery maw of the incinerator lay before them. The cubes of crushed garbage were being fed into it on a moving conveyor belt just like the sorting room.

When he dropped to the floor, he felt the extreme heat fanning his face. Shayna grabbed his hand. "There's no way out except through the fire," she whimpered.

"What if I get Eddie to turn it off?"

"He won't do it. He couldn't get the compactor to go off." Knock rolled his eyes. "He's useless."

"Don't count Eddie out." Logan sent Eddie another message. "If he can turn it off, there's probably an ash cleanout just like back on Earth. We can run through it and get out through the back."

Shayna moaned. "The crematorium, ugh! I didn't like that at all."

"This will be a little different. It'll smell worse."

"It couldn't."

Eddie's message came in and Logan read it. "He's working on it."

"At least we are not all waiting for him to do something while a giant machine tries to crush us to death." Raj rubbed his arms. "And it is warm in here."

Chapter Twenty-Two

They found a tiny space beside the conveyor belt to sit while they waited for Eddie to shut the thing down. Logan and Knock had examined every inch of the incinerator room looking for a way out or a control panel, some way to turn the thing off. Frustrated with failure, they decided to wait. "You know, there's not an unlimited supply of trash," Logan said to Shayna. "When it's processed, the incinerator should turn off. We won't have to rely on Eddie."

Knock brightened. "You could be right."

The last cube of trash disappeared into the incinerator. The automatic door clanged shut and locked, and then it got really hot. But the high temperature soon died down and the door of the incinerator popped open again.

Logan was just feeling like they should make a run for it when the compactor clicked on and the crusher wall moved back into position. When it clunked into place, they heard the unmistakable sound of garbage falling and crashing into the crusher. The crusher cranked up, chug chugging, and the compactor began spitting a fresh supply of garbage cubes onto the conveyor and the flames in the incinerator kicked on.

"Knock, next time it burns the trash and the door opens, we need to make a run for it. There's maybe three minutes before the incinerator comes back on. I tried to count, but lost it around a-hundred-fifty."

Shayna shook her head vigorously. "The floor of that thing will be too hot."

"We all have boots on," Raj said. "Even me. Logan's right. It's our only chance."

"We can wait for Eddie," she said. "I hate incinerators."

"Eddie ain't gonna do nothing." Knock's voice was full of scorn. "We can't wait here forever. I bet this place processes trash twenty-four-seven."

"Knock's right," Logan said. "We can't wait for Eddie. I'm sure he'd help if he could. Who knows what he's going through."

Eddie had just hacked into the facility's computer controls when he heard the elevators coming. He filed through rapidly searching for the compactor's controls. He got sidetracked by files containing information on the face recognition system. There was a scanner in the panel. He input his information and pressed his face against the scanner. The laser ran down and across his face and he was in the system as the elevator dinged to a stop. He had just given himself access to every part of the prison and spaceport and was hunting for the compactor again, praying he hadn't killed his friends, when the door of the elevator opened and disgorged four SS officers.

The last cube spit out of the compactor and headed into the incinerator, Logan jumped up, pulled Shayna after him and urged Raj and Knock to get ready. They waited for the incinerator to blast the rest of the garbage to cinders. When the crusher began chugging back for another run, Logan put his foot on the belt and got ready. The incinerator door opened. The flames were dying and heat blasted them. Logan's heart thumped heavily in his chest. It was going to be really hot inside.

"Now!" Logan yelled. He leapt onto the conveyor belt and shot into the incinerator. Just as he thought, there was a door on the other side. It had opened and ash was falling through it in a flood.

The floor of the incinerator was blazing hot. Logan was afraid his space boots were going to ignite as he raced across the ten feet inside the incinerator and dove through the door. Shayna tumbled after him crying out in fear and pain followed by Raj. Knock was scrambling through when the door began to close. Logan grabbed his arms and pulled him through just as the door slammed shut.

Shayna's boots were in flames. Raj's boots as well. Logan helped them snatch the burning footwear off their feet. Both had minor burns. Raj's were the worst, but he steadfastly assured Logan he was fine.

Logan examined their new surroundings. In the next room, as the compactor geared up, the walls crashed and vibrated. They were in a small concrete block room filled with reeking ashes and tarry black chunks of unburned material. When a huge vacuum suddenly began sucking the ash out of the room, Logan felt the air going with it. The vacuum must be spitting the ash onto the moon's surface. The incinerator whooshed into high and Logan felt like this was the end. In seconds, there would be no air and they would all die a horrible death.

Instinctively, Logan snapped his space suit's mask in place. Oxygen began to flow. Knock did the same. It only took a minute for him to realize he and Knock would survive, at least until their air ran out, but Raj and Shayna would die. As soon as it hit him, he unsnapped his face plate and stared at Shayna and Raj. Their eyes were bulging and they were beginning to cough and gasp for air. The suction had drawn them all toward the giant vent pipe.

"Let us go!" Shayna shouted over the noise. "Save yourself."

"No!" Logan flatly refused. "I won't leave you to die."

"It's stupid for all of us to die." She wrestled with him trying to push his face plate down and seal it. They struggled and she ended up in his arms sobbing.

Knock pushed back his mask. "Dude, if you're dying, so am I."

Logan sank to the floor. Ash swirled around them as it was sucked into the huge silver duct. "We're in this together," Knock said.

Logan pulled all three of his friends close. They huddled on the floor gasping for air as the compactor, the incinerator and the vacuum roared. Logan prepared to die. He hugged Shayna hard, closed his eyes and gave up the fight. Then all the machinery stopped at once.

Logan looked up first. "What?"

His wrist com buzzed and he lifted it to read. "Eddie. He's got everything turned off."

A clang above their heads made them all focus on the ceiling. A hatch dropped down and Eddie stuck his head through. "What're you guys waiting for?"

Logan jumped up, shoved Shayna toward Eddie who quickly pulled her and Raj through the hatch. Logan was the last to go. When they were all inside the service tube above the garbage equipment and the hatch closed, Eddie started the machinery by using a small cube he had in his hand. "Gotta keep the trash moving," he said. "You have no idea how much this place puts out."

"Eddie!" Logan pounded his friend on the back. "We thought we were goners. Where you been?"

"Dodging a million Enforcers. This place is crawling with them. I was working on turning this compactor off when four of them popped out of an elevator right in my face. I thought I was dead." He started laughing. "One of them came over to me. I had the guts out of a control panel next to the elevators and was hacking the garbage equipment. All he did was pat me on the back. He said, 'I'm glad to see someone is finally fixing the elevators. Way to go.'"

"What did you say to him then?"

"I said, yeah, the damn things are always on the fritz."

They laughed and began crawling down the tube. "It's our fault you had to deal with the SS and the Enforcers swarming the place," Logan admitted as they crawled to the end of the tube and dropped into a dark service alley. "We got caught getting off the Lift and chased around the outside of the prison."

Raj was shivering. Logan pulled his pack off and found a thin jacket. "Here, put this on before you freeze to death."

"Where are we, Eddie," Knock asked. "Got a plan to get us out of here?"

"Yeah, GPS boy, you got the map?" Eddie knocked on Logan's helmet.

Logan clicked his face mask down and keyed the map of the facility. He examined it for some time while everyone else caught their breath and rested. "I see my red dot but according to this we're still in the compactor. This section of the service tunnels must not be on the schematics. Eddie, what's this second red dot?" Logan tapped on his face mask.

"Nothing, Logan, ignore it. Plot us a course to the space port."

"We have to try for a ship?" Shayna's voice was filled with fear. "Oh no, does that mean we can't go back to Earth?"

"The Lift is out of the question," Eddie said. "This place is on lock down."

Logan tried to see Shayna in the dark. All he could make out was a wet, disheveled figure covered with a layer of white ash. They were all a mess. "We wanted to try for Earth, Shayna, but if Eddie says it's impossible, well, he knows what he's talking about."

"But if we can't go home, where will we go?"

"Eddie says there are free people building camps on most of the mining planets. We'll try to make it to one."

"Oh my God, that's insane."

"No, Shayna, off-world is going to be the only place for people who want to live free," Raj said. "My uncle, the Professor, told me that soon Earth will be covered with concrete, only a few Vagrants will be left alive, and there will be no food or water for us to live on. The Company has it planned. They want to make Earth into their homeport totally controlled by them with no dissidents allowed. They're already doing it. He's afraid they will discover some truly horrible way to do away with all of us soon. He and his friends have been planning to . . ."

"That's enough, Raj."

Logan was shocked. Eddie had stopped Raj from saying something. "What are the Professor's friends planning?"

"It's better if you don't know," Eddie said. "If you get stopped or captured, ignorance will be your savior."

"Raj knows and he's just a kid."

Eddie drew them further down the tunnel. "Like you're all grown up. You're a kid, too, Logan. You're all kids."

Shayna sobbed. "I don't understand anything you're talking about. I'm terrified. I mean, another planet? We'll never make it. Who's gonna fly the spaceship?"

Logan grabbed her in a hug and held her. "Don't freak out, girl, at least you ain't shooting out an air duct in a cloud of ash right now. Be happy we're all alive and out of that nightmare."

She nodded and rested her head on his shoulder for a minute.

Eddie went to the wall and sat down. "We need to rest and make a plan."

They all went to the wall and slid slowly to the floor huddled around Eddie. "Listen, this place is crazy alive with Enforcers and SS," he said. "They know you guys are here. They know Shayna and Raj have escaped and are running around loose. They don't know if you're all together, but they assume it and they think you'll try for the Lift, so that's why the spaceport is our only hope."

Shayna moaned and looked away.

Eddie gestured to the empty corridor. "Take a break. You have no idea how close you guys came to cashing in your tickets. I barely got the machinery stopped. I've been monitoring the chit chat on the internal channels. The SS think you guys may have been inside the compactor and hope you died, so we have a few minutes. But it won't last. They'll check for DNA in the compactor."

Knock scooted next to Eddie. "Gross, dude. You got any grub?"

Eddie pulled his pack off and started handing out Sopore-free bread and food he'd brought with him, nuts, tubes of water and energy bars made of soy, peanut butter and raisins. Knock tore a chunk of bread off and chewed lustily. "Man, I was starving."

"We're all hungry," Shayna said.

They sat eating and slurping from the water tubes for ten minutes. Logan felt if he stopped too long he'd fall asleep. He looked at Eddie's bulging pack. "What's in that thing?"

Eddie pulled it close to his chest. "Tools and stuff I need to get us out of here. We better get started soon. We gotta keep going. If we stop too long, they'll have more time to figure out where we are and where we're going."

Logan turned to Eddie. "Where are we going?"

"I have this kind of figured out. We need to free all the detainees. That will cause the maximum amount of chaos and we'll take as many as want to go and as many as we can with us. There's a freighter fueled up and waiting on the pad for a load of detainees. It's supposed to off-world to Google."

"Google?" Logan said. "What did that planet used to be called? I'm not up on all the corporate names they gave them."

"Google is Gliese, the planet where they sent your dad."

Logan sighed and started packing up the food. "That's where we think they sent him."

"There were only two worlds being mined when they captured him," Eddie said. "Gliese and Ramirez which is now Exxon. You got a fifty-fifty chance of finding him on Google."

"I can't get my hopes up like that, Eddie. And after all this time, even if it was the right planet, he's probably dead. Miners died in droves in the beginning."

Eddie shrugged. "Hey, a dream is always a good thing. Hold onto the dream, man. It's worth having. Your dad was Army. He fought in wars and he's a survivor. One day you'll be reunited with him and live happily ever after as free people. I'd kill for that dream."

Logan laughed as he pulled himself to his feet. "It is a good dream, Eddie, but just a dream."

Shayna grabbed his arm. "I believe," she said. "I think it's a dream that can come true."

Eddie patted her arm. "That's right, tell him it can happen. I'd give anything to be able to see my father and live free. Hell, I'd do anything to have a father." He burst out laughing. "So we're all gonna hop on your dream, Logan. Lead on."

Chapter Twenty-Three

"We need to access the air ducts," Eddie said as they packed up and prepared to leave. "There's an entire system of huge air ducts under the facility I couldn't see on the diagrams and schematics we had. When I accessed the system, I discovered it."

Logan stood up and stretched. "Okay, lead on."

"Air ducts?" Knock said.

Eddie led them down the dark alley to a locked room. It was locked with facial recognition software. Eddie crammed his face against the plate, the scanner read it and the door clicked. Eddie looked both ways down the alley and slipped inside. They followed him into a room filled with air scrubbers, vents and huge gray metal boxes containing make-air systems. The machinery kicked on and roared. Eddie walked right to an access door in the ceiling, boosted himself up and disappeared. Logan lifted Raj and Shayna and then Knock jumped up and pulled the door closed after him.

The duct was as big as a subway tunnel. Forced air roared around them. Logan's hair blew and Raj had to button his jacket to keep from getting it ripped off. It was like standing in a hurricane.

Eddie consulted a diagram etched into the door panel. "That way," he yelled and pointed down the duct to the left. Thankfully, that was the way the air was blowing. Logan didn't think they could fight the head winds for long. Talking was impossible. They ran with the wind blowing them at a faster pace than they might have been able to maintain without the help. When they came to a crossroads, Eddie stopped. The air was whistling out of the duct on the left. Eddie consulted another diagram, holding his pack tightly to his chest to keep from losing it. Logan examined the diagram imprinted on a plate affixed to one of the walls in the crossroads over Eddie's shoulder.

Eddie traced one of the ducts to the detainee holding area with his finger and glanced at Logan. Logan nodded and they turned left into the strong wind. It was tough going. They fought to keep moving, leaning into the massive air flow. At one point it grew so cold there was snow flying into their faces. It took them a lot longer to cover the same ground and they arrived at a hatch exhausted and chilled to the bone. Eddie used Logan's Level-Five key to open the hatch and they dropped into the roar of another room containing oxygen-generating equipment.

Logan went to the door with Eddie. He opened it and they looked out together. They were in a dark service alley. Logan heard dishes clattering and pans clanging. He smelled food. Raj stuck his head out with them and pointed. "Cafeteria," he said right into Logan's ear.

Logan nodded. This was where things were going to get dicey. Eddie wanted to free the detainees and Logan agreed it was the best plan. But how?

When the make-air equipment clicked off, Eddie drew Logan into a corner. "I'm gonna try to unlock the place," he said softly. "I'll message you when I've got the doors to the hallways outside the cafeteria opened. This is the best time to try to alert all the detainees that they are free. You know, while they're all in here. When I get the doors unlocked, you guys run through the cafeteria, throw the doors open and scream, 'We're free!' That oughta send the detainees running for the exits. You guys hide in the crowd and make your way to the service tunnel leading underground to the spaceport."

Logan pulled up the schematics of the facility and located the tunnel to the spaceport. He spotted an elevator leading down behind the kitchens. "I don't wanna risk Shayna and Raj," he whispered. "Me and Knock will do the risky stuff. I'll leave Raj and Shayna where it's safe by the elevators." He pointed to a mop room on his helmet's map. "Here."

Eddie nodded. "Let's hope this uniform gets me through the cafeteria." He shook Logan's hand and hugged him. "Good luck."

"You, too. You'll meet us at the spaceport?"

Eddie nodded. "If I'm not there, board the Far Horizon, commandeer it and wait for me. It's docked on the other side of the ice ships."

"Ice ships?"

"They bring in huge chunks of ice from the asteroid belt and melt them for drinking water. Some of it even goes back to Earth."

"I didn't know."

"Oh yeah, space ice supplies all of New York with drinking water."

"How are we supposed to take over the ship?"

Eddie took a blaster out of his pack and handed it to Logan. "Use this."

Logan stared at the evil weapon. It used laser technology to burn up anyone in the path of its beam. It also contained small projectiles filled with explosive gas that could blow up a city block and anything in it. "Where will you be?"

Eddie looked off into the distance and Logan felt like he was thinking about what to say. "I have something I need to do. The Professor sent me on a mission. The less you know the better. Just know this, if I succeed, Earth will be free of Sopore."

Logan shook his head. "What in the heck are you talking about?"

"Your dad was working on something with the Professor and we're finally ready to put it into action. Keep the faith, man. I'll see you soon."

"I don't understand. Dad was working on something with the Professor?"

"Take care of these guys, Logan. Your dad was a hero."

Logan nodded and Eddie patted his shoulder. "You'll be fine," he said as he slipped out and Logan sat down to wait.

Logan outlined the plan to Shayna, Raj and Knock before the air machinery clicked back on and made talking impossible. Shayna clung to him like she'd never see him again. He had to be strong for her so he hugged her and smiled. She laid her head on his shoulder and he felt like if he could find his father and build a life on another planet, it would be wonderful as long as she was with him.

It wasn't long until he got the message from Eddie. "The doors are unlocked. Let's go."

He led Raj and Shayna to the mop room, opened it with his Level-Five key and pushed them inside. "Wait for us. We shouldn't be long."

"What do we do if you don't come back?" Shayna cried. "How will we know what's happened to you?"

"Leave the door ajar," Logan said. "When you hear screaming, you'll know we got the doors open."

Shayna clung to him, her eyes wide with fright. Logan didn't know how to reassure her. He was pretty freaked out himself. "Let's go," he hissed to Knock. Knock nodded and they slipped into the crowd of detainees eating and talking in small groups throughout the crowded cafeteria. They were dressed strangely in their space suits. The black neoprene stuck out like a turd floating in a punchbowl filled with gray jumpsuits. Logan felt like a bug on a glass slide. Everyone was looking at them.

He grabbed Knock's arm. "Run!"

Two guards and an enforcer had spotted them and raced across the cafeteria. The enormous number of detainees blocked the guards' path, but Logan and Knock knew they were in trouble. They began dropping anyone in their way as they rushed the doors. Knock used his shoulders to throw people wearing gray left and right.

Banks of locked doors covered one long wall. Each door led into the hall. This was how they marched the transportees out and to the waiting ships. Logan hit the first one. It opened and he screamed. "Run for it! We're free."

Knock threw open the next door. Logan kept screaming while he jumped up and down and waved his arms. "We're free! We're free!"

The crowd in the cafeteria must be doped to the eyeballs on Sopore, because it took them forever to notice him, but they finally picked up on his screaming and yelling and came alive. As one, the enormous mass of humanity, men, women and children alike, charged the doors. A surging, shrieking wave of gray humans hit the doors and flowed through to freedom screaming like banshees. Chaos ensued.

Their job done, all they had to do was get back to Shayna and Raj behind the kitchens. Knock and Logan flowed into the mass in the hallway, ran for a couple of yards and then turned back into the cafeteria through the open doors. Logan held his hand out to stop Knock. "See the guards?"

Knock stood tall and scanned the cafeteria over the heads of the fleeing detainees. "Looks like one of them is down." He pointed to a spot where the flood of prisoners flowed around something on the floor.

"See the other two?"

Knock shook his head. "No, let's do it."

They skirted the edge of the gigantic room, avoiding the masses of detainees shoving and pushing toward the open doors. Alarms sounded and Logan looked at Knock. A small herd of Enforcers and guards carrying riot shields and cattle prods erupted from the kitchens and attacked the rear of the mass of detainees struggling to escape. Screams and shouts filled the room with a cacophony of dissonant noise as Logan and Knock made their way around the room, leaped over the serving counter, and dived through the double swinging doors into the kitchen. They didn't stop or slow down. Most of the kitchen help had fled toward freedom. The kitchens were empty.

A guard spotted them and Logan and Knock paused. "What's going on out there?"

Logan held up the badge hanging from the lanyard around his neck. "The doors popped open. It's hell, man. The detainees are all over the place. They're out, man. They're running for it. Orders are for space suits. They're afraid upstairs that the prisoners will blow the airlocks."

The guard looked thoughtful for a moment and said to his buddy. "I think there's a locker with suits on Level One. We better get one before they're all gone."

The two guards took off in another direction and Logan and Knock exited the kitchen speedily making their way to the mop room. Logan threw open the door and Shayna launched herself into his arms. "Whoa! We aren't safe yet."

"I was afraid you'd never come back." She pointed to Raj who now wore a chef's hat and two aprons. "He needs clothes."

Raj waved his hand. "Don't worry about me. Let's get to the Far Horizon."

"Did you let everyone out?" Shayna asked as Logan hit the button calling the elevator.

Knock leaned forward. "It's a screaming riot out there."

"How many got out?" Raj asked while they waited.

"I don't know." Logan pressed his ear to the elevator doors. "I don't think this is working. They must have shut the elevators down."

Shayna moaned. "Now what do we do?"

Logan was stunned. When he dropped his face mask and pulled up the GPS, he saw nothing useful nearby.

Shayna suddenly perked up. "Stairwell," she said. "There's always a stairwell next to the elevators."

"This isn't the mall," Knock said.

But Shayna was on the hunt. Logan tried to stop her. "There is no stairwell. I checked the map."

She moved along the wall with a purpose, stopping about twenty feet away. She pointed. "See? I told you."

Logan couldn't believe it. There was a stairwell clearly marked with the word Stairs. The door was locked. Logan tried to use his key to open it. It didn't work.

"Facial recognition only," Raj said as he pointed to the reader embedded in the wall.

"Stand back!" Logan commanded, took the blaster out of his pack and pointed it at the door. Logan didn't know what Eddie counted an emergency. He just knew this was starting to feel like one. He pointed the blaster at the lock and hit the trigger. A blinding blast of light shot out of the weapon and the door exploded.

"Let's go!" Knock shouted and shot through the smoking aperture.

As they pounded down the steps, Logan prayed they wouldn't meet guards, SS or Enforcers coming up. He held the blaster ready to fire just in case. They hit the bottom of the stairwell and Logan opened the door slowly. He checked the corridor and saw no one. "Eddie was right. Chaos upstairs, no Enforcers down here."

Chapter Twenty-Four

Eddie had come on this trip to the moon with a mission. He'd allowed Logan to think he was here only to help him rescue Shayna and Raj. In reality, he was here for the Professor and all Vagrants and free people. The Company had to go down.

In his pack, Eddie carried ten vials of an anti-Sopore cleansing agent so powerful, if he dropped it into the water supply, all residents of New Washington who drank the water would be Sopore free, and stay Sopore free for a month. The Professor had reasoned that the drug made the Company capable of governing masses of people it didn't have the personnel or the manpower to govern any other way. The Company was stretched very thin. Its operations in outer space took precedence. The good soldiers, the strong guards, Enforcers and SS were on other planets and the moon preventing uprisings and keeping the flow of gold, precious gems and metals flowing into the Company coffers. If the people were suddenly Sopore free and couldn't get doped on Sopore for a long period of time, they would see the tyranny and revolt against it. When that happened, the Vagrants would join them and overthrow the Company.

Even if the Professor's plan didn't work, it would shake the status quo on Earth and on the moon in a major way. Eddie was committed to making the plan work even if it meant sacrificing his life to succeed.

When he left Logan, he made his way through the secret subterranean ways beneath the floor of the lunar facility. His goal was a water treatment and processing center. Logan's father's Three-D map of the facility had given the Professor the information he'd been searching for. Declan Hall had been committed to this project before he was picked up and deported. He'd stolen the Three-D map cube and hidden it. With this map, the Professor had seen where the treatment plant was located and how to access it.

Ships towing huge frozen-water asteroids, docked them in the plant. The icebergs were heated and the melting water processed, cleaned, sterilized and stored in gigantic tanks on the moon's surface. The water was then pumped into huge tanker ships run by the Tong and shipped to Earth. The prison was also on the pipeline getting all its freshwater from the tanks. There were six of them.

Eddie trotted along on the access tunnel which looked a lot like a subway tunnel with no tracks. He saw no guards and no SS. They were all busy trying to round up a thousand crazed detainees. Eddie smiled. That part of the plan had been fun. The tunnel ended in an airlock. There was a small room beside it containing space suits. Eddie took a modern neoprene moon suit down and pulled it on. He plucked a fully-charged air capsule off a shelf filled with them, plugged one into his suit and tossed three spares into his pack. When his face plate was down, he sucked in the processed air and plunged through the first door of the airlock, waited while the next door activated then exited to the surface.

This was the dicey part of the plan, but Eddie was committed. He'd spent most of his life fighting against Sopore. His mother had died of an overdose in the early days when the Company was just starting to infuse all food with it. Now people knew better than to drink ten sodas in an hour or eat an entire cake. At least most people knew better.

On the moon's surface, Eddie hiked in huge bounding strides toward the spaceport. He did his best to keep low, but it was hard. There was so little gravity on the moon, too big a leap might take him into space. The tanks were located outside the main facility. He spotted the transport ship Far Horizon on the other side of the iceberg docks and hoped Logan and the kids would make it. They deserved a break. Eddie was committed to this plan. If he lived, he'd join Logan. If he died, it didn't matter. He'd dedicated his life to obliterating Sopore and freeing Earth from the tyranny of the Company. If he died, it would be fighting for a cause he believed in.

The water treatment facility was a bizarre structure built around huge docks for the icebergs. Large gray, black and blue chunks of frozen water and suspended matter stuck out of the docks slowly dissolving into the treatment plant. As they dissolved enormous clouds of water vapor built around the chunks of ice, creating a mini atmosphere. The puffy clouds had spread to the tanks. As Eddie bounded by, it started raining on him.

The water containment tanks rose off the moon surface as big as football stadiums, each one filled with millions of gallons of water. The tanks were Eddie's goal. He bounded by the two iceberg docks on this side of the plant and headed for a ladder climbing the side of the first tank. So far, no one had spotted him. He looked like any other prison employee out to maintain equipment wearing the Company's space suit.

The climb up the side of the tank would be his most dangerous position and he had to do it six times. Halfway up the first tank, he had an anxiety attack and had to stop and slow his breathing. If he sucked down all his air too soon, he wouldn't finish. With his fear under control, he glanced around the facility from his high perch. He didn't see a single guard or enforcer. The riot had all of them safely occupied. He saw activity around some of the ships, but the Far Horizon seemed deserted. It sat in its cradle like a gigantic silver whale. Lights on the side of the ship blinked, but the windows of the helm were opaque.

He completed the climb and bounced wildly across the broad gray metal surface until he came to a round, locked access. It responded to his badge and clunked open. Eddie smiled, facial recognition was not viable in space but he had been prepared. He lifted the heavy opening with both hands. When he shined a light into the dark interior, he saw water right up to the top. It only took a minute to grab a vial from his pack. He held the precious liquid, carefully prepared back on Earth by the Professor, in his hands for a moment and said a prayer, then he dumped it into the water. With the port locked down again, he scoped out the second tank. It looked close enough to jump to. He got a running start, leaped high and shot across the sixty feet separating the tanks. For a moment, he thought he might just keep going, but he was able to land before he fell off the other side. Laughing and breathing a little too fast, he spiked that tank and moved on to the next. When he was finished, he plugged in a fresh cylinder of air, sat back to rest and messaged Logan to find out where they were.

****

Logan and Knock found the service alley leading to the spaceport quickly. The place was deserted. He led his friends down it at a run. They were tired, but the end of their journey in sight renewed their energy. When they came to an airlock, they stopped. "Now what?" Shayna said as she gasped for air after their run.

Knock grabbed Logan's arm. "Space suits."

Logan remembered the room they'd found at the bottom of the exhaust tube they'd trashed. It seemed like years ago. The room had been next to an airlock and it had been filled with space suits. He used his Level-Five key to open the door Knock indicated and sure enough it was filled with suits and canisters of compressed air.

Shayna took a suit off the wall and looked at it with disgust. "This has been worn before."

Logan sighed. "I know, but it's all we have."

Shayna sniffed. "I don't like the way it smells."

"Just put it on," Raj snapped. "We're trying to get out of here in a hurry. Do not be so fussy. We have no time."

Shayna reluctantly pulled the suit on, starting with the feet. When she had it up to her waist, she stopped and held out her hands in a gesture of helpless supplication. "Now what?"

Logan laughed stepped over to her and held one arm while she slipped into it, and then the other. He handed her the gloves and sealed them over her wrists. She needed more help with fastening the seals around her neck and shoulders. When it was tight, Logan handed her the helmet and mask. She smiled hesitantly into his face. "Thanks. I don't mean to be difficult."

"You're fine," he said. "You're just nervous and scared. We all are."

"You're scared?"

He smiled as he helped her put the helmet over her hair. "Out of my mind."

"You'd never know," she said. "You seem so sure of yourself and so . . . well brave."

"I have to be. I have no choice. The only other option is unthinkable. That's failure. I came here to get you and Raj and take you to safety and that's what I plan to do." He pulled her close, a difficult maneuver in space suits, and kissed her. "You'll be fine."

She nodded ruefully. "This suit still smells like a cat used it for a sandbox."

"Breath shallowly."

Logan handed her a pair of space boots. She stared into them. "These smell worse than the suit."

Logan shrugged. "People sweat."

Raj needed help with sealing his suit. When Logan had him in, he said, "That should do."

With Shayna and Raj suited up, Knock and Logan resupplied with fresh air cylinders, they set off through the airlock and onto the surface of the moon.

Shayna stopped outside and stared. Earth glowed like a beautiful blue and green gem hanging in a black velvet sky. Clouds drifted across the gemlike surface of their home planet and Logan wondered if he would ever set foot on it again. Its beauty was enough to strike anyone dumb with awe, but they were in a hurry. He grabbed her arm and she followed him. Ahead, a wide gravel road led to a cluster of deep space ships and moon shuttles waiting to take off. Machines on tracks ground along the road pulling tanks of fuel and water, and trailers of supplies and freight.

Logan keyed his comm. "We need to avoid them. Some might be manned. Some are run by robots."

Knock nodded and turned off the track. They would have to go around the water tanks and come up on the space ships from the rear. As they slid between two gigantic steel tanks, Logan wondered where Eddie was. They stopped at the edge of the water tanks to look for SS or guards and he saw the docking area for ice asteroids. Logan tapped on Knock's shoulder and pointed. The Far Horizon was on the other side of the iceberg docks. A swarm of workers in space suits were busy loading the ship. They would have to get through them somehow to board, then they would have to find Eddie.

They were walking under an asteroid being drained of its water when he got Eddie's message. Logan sent him one saying they were close to the Far Horizon but there were workers present. Eddie said to stop before they got to the ship and he would meet them.

Logan sent him a "roger that," message and waved to his friends to follow him. They stayed in the shadow of the giant iceberg as they slipped closer to the Far Horizon, a Class D space cruiser. The ship rested in a cradle with wires attached to keep it stable and to provide power, pipes filling it with fuel and more pipes sending water into the ship's reservoirs. Huge hatches in the side were open and being filled with pallets of supplies by men using human-driven robotic cargo loaders. The robots clanked around on jointed legs, lifting the pallets with fork-lift arms. From this angle, Logan could see the massive burners of the two great engines in the rear of the ship.

Logan was about to move closer when Knock laid a restraining hand on his arm and shook his head. He pointed and Logan turned to see a moon buggy leap a hill, land with a bounce and shoot toward the ship. Two SS sat in the seat. They waited while the men in the buggy conversed with the men loading. Pretty soon it became clear they were sending the loading crew back to the prison. Maybe they needed extra help catching the escaped prisoners. Logan turned and stared across the surface toward the prison and saw a horde of escaped detainees flowing out of the facility. All wore space suits and Logan wondered where they'd found that many, but he clapped Knock on the back and raised a triumphant fist. If he hadn't been wearing a suit, he would have cheered.

Suddenly, a small figure ran toward the escaping detainees. The new figure stopped the detainees and motioned toward the Far Horizon. Logan keyed his comm. "That has to be Eddie."

Shayna elbowed between him and Knock. "Is Eddie helping them?"

"He must be," Raj said. "Who else would risk their life to help those poor people?"

Knock keyed the com unit. "You know, I never thought of Eddie as being brave."

Logan shrugged. "We just didn't look hard enough."

As they held their breath, Eddie gathered the escapees around him. Logan could see the SS in the buggy headed for him along with several cargo loaders in their gigantic robots. Eddie pushed the milling crowd toward the water tanks and the waiting ship. It was like they were moving in slow motion.

"We need to help him!" Shayna cried.

"Let's go," Knock called and started running back toward the facility.

Logan followed at a bounding run. His jumps carried him halfway up the side of the water tanks. While he and Knock ran, he keyed the com and told Shayna and Raj to wait. They met the first wave of the detainees on the other side of the tanks and motioned for them to follow. Eddie was too far back for Logan to see.

With the detainees following, Logan turned toward the Far Horizon. "Logan, look!" Knock yelled into the comm.

Logan followed Knock's pointing finger and gasped. "What the heck is that?"

One of the detainees, a large man in an aged first-gen space suit spoke into the comm. "They're the new robotic moon Enforcers. We've all seen them before. They shoot some kind of laser and are programmed to kill detainees."

"Holy crap!" Logan whispered. Coming around the corner of the massive prison facility were three twelve-foot tall robots with a flat dish-like object balanced on top of segmented legs. The dish seemed to be the control center. A blue light flicked back and forth across a narrow band on its front. The robots moved fast in the low gravity and were headed right for them.

"Run!" Logan screamed into his com unit.

Knock took off, headed back toward Raj and Shayna with a stream of detainees following. Logan stayed behind to help funnel the mass of detainees after him toward the Far Horizon. Suddenly Eddie appeared. He tapped on Logan's shoulder and indicated Logan should leave as one of the robot Enforcers fired a blue beam into the group of detainees. A detainee instantly exploded in a pyre of blue flames. Stunned, Logan turned to Eddie.

"What was that?"

"I have no idea, but it's bad, really bad," Eddie returned. "Lead these guys to safety."

Logan felt panic rising in his chest like a tide of lava. "What are you gonna do?"

Eddie shrugged. "I got no idea, but I'll think of something. Now go!"

He pushed Logan which sent him into the air. Logan looked back over his shoulder as he landed and saw Eddie run out in front of one of the robotic Enforcers and wave his arms. He keyed his comm. "Knock, take Shayna and Raj and these prisoners and run for the ship. There's no one guarding it. Now is your chance."

"What about you?"

"Eddie is trying to decoy the killer robots. He needs help. I gotta do it, Knock. He saved us. I owe him."

Knock didn't try to convince him not to help Eddie. He knew better. He banged his face mask on Logan's. "Be safe, dude. See you on the ship."

Before he could get away, Shayna grabbed Logan's hand. "Don't do it," she said in a tear-filled voice. "Don't Logan. I'll never see you again."

He brushed her off. "I have to. Don't try to stop me. I'd never forgive myself."

He pushed her toward Knock and took off in a bounding run toward the killer robots shooting blue fire at the mass of detainees.

Chapter Twenty-Five

Logan made sure Shayna went with Knock and Raj and then turned to help Eddie. His heart pounded in his throat but he was remarkably calm. Once he had made the decision, all his fear melted away.

Eddie had the attention of the robots. They charged after him on their odd jointed legs and big metal feet as he bounced wildly toward the water tanks. They didn't see Logan coming up behind them which was all part of Logan's fantastic plan. He leaped high and clambered on top of a row of buildings edging the road to the spaceport. He ran down the rooftops until he found a spot on top of an open building used for storing the cargo loaders. He stopped, took a deep breath and braced himself. He would have only one chance to do this. He couldn't miss.

He took the blaster out of his pack and sighted on one of the huge monster machines chasing Eddie. As the last one rounded the corner of the row of buildings, he saw Eddie didn't have a prayer unless Logan could pull off a miracle. When he felt like he couldn't miss, he fired the blaster. The explosive charge slung him backward twenty feet and off the roof. He fell flat and bounced. Low gravity had some really positive attributes.

He was behind the building so he never saw his shot hit the last robot chasing Eddie. He slowly climbed to his feet and ran around the side of the building. His shot had blown off a section of the robot's leg. As Logan ran for it, the robot wobbled once and then collapsed in the middle of firing. The blue bolt caught the robot in front of it and blew it to bits. Only one hideous robot remained and it had a bead on Eddie and was closing in.

Logan knew he would never catch it in time. He was still trying to recover from getting knocked silly. Firing a blaster in this low gravity was an insane thing to do. He watched helplessly as he scrambled and bounded forward as fast as he could to regain lost ground. The robot rained blue fire on Eddie as he raced for the cover of the tanks. Eddie was just rounding the corner of the first tank when a bolt of blue broadsided the tank and blew half of it off. The metal side fell toward Eddie and Logan froze. The robot fired again and the side of the tank falling toward Eddie exploded, sending a shower of metal shards everywhere. Eddie was hit and went down hard.

A flood of water exploded from the tank. Droplets froze and turned to snow. The main body of water took longer but after the first gush, it too froze, but not until it had encompassed the robot. The huge machine was frozen for a few moments while Logan rushed to find Eddie. The grinding gears and servo-motors in the robot's legs sounded like they were about to explode. Steam rose from around it along with smoke. Logan smelled burning oil and metal.

When the robot finally broke free, a huge chunk of ice shattered and flew everywhere. A gigantic shard of ice tore into the control pod of the robot and stuck there. It began turning in crazy circles. The hole in its control pod showed blue screens and a red eye.

There was no time to enjoy the spectacle. Eddie was under the ice. Logan took bounding leaps trying to cover the ground separating them as fast as possible. He only had a few minutes before Eddie's suit deflated and all his air was sucked out.

Crazy for some way to get Eddie out from under the ton of ice that had formed over him, Logan spotted the cargo loaders. He'd never run one, but how hard could it be? The loaders were human-controlled robotic machines with arms like the forks on a fork lift, robot legs and a control seat. Logan spotted the built-in ladder and clambered into the seat. He found the power switch and turned the machine on. It roared into life with a huge engine located behind the seat. He fit his hands into the control gloves and flexed his fingers. The forks went up and down with his hand movements. The forks had a grasper on the end that operated with finger movements. He studied the control panel for a second, figured out how to make it walk and took off out of the storage barn.

The water from the tank had frozen almost as soon as it flowed out of the tank. As minutes flew by, Logan's hope of saving Eddie faded, but he had to try. He had his robot step over the carcass of the attack robot and used his hand controls to try to lift the ice. He tore off a hunk and was mildly excited by the results. He continued chipping away at the ice mass until he spotted Eddie's foot. The water had apparently flowed over him and froze encasing him inside the mass of ice.

Logan used his machine to chip away at the chunk until he felt afraid of tearing into Eddie. Eddie's legs and head were free of the ice. Logan could see Eddie's face under the mask. His eyes were closed. There seemed to be no hope, but Logan refused to abandon his friend. Even if he managed to free him, the blue fire had pierced his suit. Eddie should be dead from loss of pressure and lack of oxygen.

Refusing to give up no matter how hopeless his cause, he climbed off the machine and carefully walked across a sheet of glare ice to grab Eddie's legs. The skin of Eddie's space suit had a substance on it to ensure the suit's seal. It was a little slippery. Logan was able to move Eddie a little and that tiny bit of movement instilled a germ of hope inside Logan. He wiggled Eddie, tried to roll him, and gradually loosened him inside his ice coffin. Tugging and pulling, Logan worked up a sweat. Eddie's torso pulled free all at once and Logan went flying as Eddie shot out of the entrapment and slid across a slick sheet of ice on the ground to stop at the foot of Logan's loader.

Gasping and out of breath from his exertions, Logan scampered up the ladder into the loader and lowered the forks. He climbed back down and grabbed Eddie's arm to pull him onto the forks. He settled Eddie on top of them and was straightening his torso when Eddie's eyes flew open. Logan backed away so fast, he slipped and fell, scrambled to his feet and skated to Eddie's head.

"Eddie! You alive?" He tapped on his friend's face plate.

Eddie's eyes fluttered. His nod was barely perceptible. Holy crap! Eddie's suit was pierced. Logan knew that. The water flowing over it and freezing must have resealed it. Eddie was still alive. "I'm taking you to the Far Horizon. Hold on, buddy."

When Shayna, Knock and Raj parted company with Logan, Shayna hesitated. He'd told her to go with Knock and take the detainees to the Far Horizon, but she felt abandoned. Even though she knew Logan was going to help his friend and wasn't leaving her, she hated to see him bounding away alone. After watching him for a few moments, Knock grabbed her arm. He keyed the comm. "Shayna, let's go. We need to move out now!"

She let him turn her and began slowly to motivate in the direction of the space ship. She could see it winking silver in the light cast by Earth. The detainees gathered around them followed as Knock led them toward the ship across the gray rocky surface of the moon. The ship sat in a crater filled with refueling equipment, fuel tanks, pallets of supplies wrapped in plastic and two other ships. One of those big ships was attached to refueling lines. The other sat in its cradle.

Lights blinked from the portholes of the Far Horizon and the ship being refueled. The cargo hatch was still hanging open though no robot loaders moved cargo anywhere in the crater. Across the top of the crater, the black sky twinkled with a million stars. Shayna shivered. Soon, they would take off into the unknown; shooting into the void headed for one of those bright lights with Eddie at the controls. That, of course, depended on Logan bringing Eddie back with him.

She keyed the comm. "Knock, who's going to fly the space ship if Logan doesn't bring Eddie back?"

"Don't think about stuff like that, Shayna. You'll only get yourself worked up over something that hasn't happened yet. We got enough problems without you inventing one. Look!" He pointed behind them.

She looked over her shoulder and gasped. Three huge robots shooting blue fire were after Eddie.

"Run!" Knock screamed into his com unit, grabbed her hand and began bounding toward the ship.

They dropped into the crater and had to jump over thick fuel lines stretched across the crater floor in every direction. She glanced off toward the space port and leaped into Knock, sending him cartwheeling. When he stopped, she grabbed his gloved hand and pointed. A moon buggy leaped the crater rim and sped down the sloping north wall headed right for them.

He pushed her ahead of him. "Get on board the ship. Take them!" He pointed to the milling detainees who seemed to have no idea of where they should go or what they should do. Many were children, but Sopore had turned the adults into children as well. Knock shoved her toward them one more time and then bounded off waving like a madman to attract the attention of the buggy driver.

Motivated, Shayna raced for the ship. Raj waved his arms to indicate to the escapees they should follow him. Some he had to actually turn toward the ship and push. When she reached the ship, Shayna stopped to examine her options. A self-propelled set of boarding stairs squatted next to one of the ship's many ports. Praying the port would be open, she flew up the steps. When she lifted the bar to unlock the door, it refused to budge. The thing was locked. Shayna wanted to cry, but there was no time. A laser bolt hit one of the detainees. The escaped prisoner burst into flames and disintegrated which caused the mass of detainees to scatter in every direction. Poor Raj ran around stopping them and pointing them back toward the ship as another wave of the escapees crested the crater rim and poured toward the ship.

Shayna swallowed her sobs, climbed the stair rail and jumped. She landed close to the cargo door, climbed into the vast hold, which was over half filled with supplies, and waved to Raj. He saw her and started pushing his childlike charges toward the open hold doors.

There was an elevator in the center of the hold. Shayna stared at it with horror and shuddered. Her memories of taking the Lift from Earth to the moon had increased an already strong phobia. She doubted whether she could get on the elevator. The detainees poured into the hold. She ran to the doors and directed them to the elevator. Fifty fit into the huge lift. They crammed inside of it behind Raj. The rest milled around the hold and hugged each other as they waited for the elevator to come back for another load.

Her job was done. She'd led them into the ship now Raj could deal with them. She jumped out of the hold and spotted Knock leading the SS away from the Far Horizon. He waved his hand to her indicating she should run. She spun around looking for Eddie and Logan and spotted a huge robot cargo loader racing toward the Far Horizon. In its carrying arms lay a space-suited figure. Either Eddie was driving and Logan in the forks or Eddie was in the forks and Logan driving. Her heart jumped and she prayed Logan was the driver.

The robot covered ground rapidly moving behind the SS in the moon buggy and catching up. It's weighted, segmented legs were more suitable than balloon tires for moon travel.

Knock spotted the cargo robot at the same time Shayna did. He took an abrupt turn and raced for it. The moon buggy slewed around sending up a wave of moon gravel which did not settle but continued to rise in a cloud of dangerously sharp pellets. When the buggy finished its turn it was right in the center of the flying gravel. Pellets and gravel particles shredded the spacesuits of the two SS in the buggy. Shayna watched with horror as the buggy crashed into a pallet of shrink-wrapped cargo spilling the two SS onto the surface of the crater. The oxygen escaping from their suits was visible as thin streamers of white. There were literally hundreds of the streamers issuing from the suits. The two SS fell onto their backs kicking and Shayna looked away.

She found Knock talking to Logan who was driving the cargo robot. Relief flooded Shayna when she saw Logan was okay. The two cut off their conversation and headed for the Far Horizon and Shayna bounded after them. When Logan and Knock reached the ship, they off-loaded Eddie. Shayna ran up in time to see Logan and Knock carrying Eddie into the ship and followed them. Knock hit a big red button on the wall and the big cargo doors began to close.

"Get Eddie topside," Logan yelled into the comm.

Shayna ran to help Knock carry Eddie into the elevator. Between them, they were able to muscle his inert weight into the huge lift. Logan followed and hit the elevator button to close the door and go up. It happened so fast Shayna had no time to be terrified. The lift was slow anyway, nothing like the elevators at home. It rose to the first level of the ship and the doors opened to chaos. Hundreds of detainees were bombarding Raj with questions he couldn't answer. Logan ripped off his helmet and held out his hands to quiet the crowd.

"People, friends, you are free! This ship has been officially taken over by Vagrants. We're getting off the moon."

The crowd cheered and crowded close.

"Everyone needs to find a blast couch and strap in." He turned to Shayna. "Take them to the passenger hold and tell them to strap in for takeoff."

Shayna grabbed his arm. "Who's gonna drive?"

"We can do this, Shayna," he whispered. "Don't freak out the crowd."

She glanced around her at the people from the detention facility. A small girl came up and took her hand. "Remember me, Miss Shayna?"

She knelt and hugged Cressy. "Of course I do. I'm so glad you're here."

"Where are we gonna go?"

"Somewhere wonderful," she said.

"Really?"

She hugged the girl again. "Yes, really."

Determined not to allow her fear to infect the children and adults gathered in the hallways and the open eating area of the ship, she smiled and leaned over to whisper to Logan. "Where's the passenger hold?"

Chapter Twenty-Six

Logan and Knock dragged Eddie into the ship's hospital. The place was depressingly dark and quiet. Logan switched on the light and surveyed the scene. "There," he said and pointed to something that looked like a plastic coffin.

Knock knelt next to Eddie and began stripping off his suit. "What's wrong with him?" Knock asked.

"Not sure. He got knocked for a loop and covered with ice. Maybe a concussion. I don't think the blue laser hit him or his suit would be blackened. Probably hypothermia." Logan put his head on Eddie's thin chest. He heard a weak slow heartbeat skip and then start again."

"Did you hear anything?" Knock hovered uncertainly.

"Get him into the Re-Juve. It's his only hope."

Together they hoisted Eddie's inert body into the coffin-like piece of equipment. Logan knew about them from the Professor. When all his limbs were inside, Logan searched for the controls. He slapped a swinging panel on the side. It lit and he hit a button helpfully labeled *Auto*.

Knock leapt out of the way as the stretcher and Eddie slid into the plastic coffin and the lid locked down. They watched for a second as thick light green fog filled the inside surrounding and covering Eddie. When they could no longer see their friend, Logan slapped Knock. "Let's roll. We got a ship to fly."

Knock followed him out and into the hall as Logan ran for the bridge. There was one central hallway in the space ship running its length. Logan prayed this was the right path to the bridge as he ran. An airlock stopped him at the end of the hall. They went through it together and popped out in the control room. Blast and meteorite protected windows ran around the room filled with computers all blinking red. Terrified he wouldn't be able to figure it out, Logan ran from one bank of holo screens to another. He found the captain's chair and slammed into it while Knock walked slowly around the room examining everything.

He stopped at a station labeled *Docking*. "Dude, I think this might be where the pilot puts this tank into the dock."

Logan hadn't found anything even remotely useful in the captain's area. He ran to see what Knock was talking about. There was a control console joystick like one of Eddie's computer games only heavier and more important looking. He quickly scanned the holo screen saw a choice on the menu for release. "Should I hit it?"

Knock shrugged. "Go for it, dude."

Logan touched the screen and another menu came up. "Whoa!" A diagram of the ship showed each cable connecting it to the moon. Logan touched them one at a time. Each time he hit a cable, the ship shuddered.

"We're gonna float out of here any minute," Knock said with real fear in his eyes.

Logan looked to the next station. "Keep hitting the cables. I'm going to hunt for an engine control."

He found the engine station. It had three seats and was a cockpit filled with holo screens. He went down two steps and walked right through one of the screens to sit in the middle seat. There was a place for a key. He stuck his Level-Five key into it and a low rumble shook the ship. Lights and gauges blazed all around him and he remembered driving the fancy car out of New Jersey. "Knock, are all the cables released?"

"Yes," Knock whispered. "Look."

Logan glanced out the window and saw the moon slowly receding. "Holy crap! Now what?"

"Start the freaking engines."

"How?"

"Just tell them to start. Maybe they will like cars."

"Engines start," Logan yelled. Immediately the low rumble turned into a roar and the huge ship began moving away from the moon straight toward Earth.

Frantic, Logan left that station and ran to the captain's seat and buckled in. A new holoscreen had opened up with choices. He saw Gliese 667, Exon, Kepler 22b, Tau Ceti and Monsonta. He recognized them as mining worlds. Closing his eyes, he prayed for the first time in his life. Not to the Professor's weird gods but to his idea of an all-powerful father. He prayed he was making the right choice as he touched Gliese 667.

The minute he touched the symbol on the holo screen, his chair began wrapping around his body, pinning him tightly. "Logan, I can't move," Knock screamed.

"I think the ship is in control now, dude. Just hang on."

"Oh crap, I hope you're right."

The chair slowly covered Logan with blue foam. When he was encased, he felt calm and closed his eyes. He was almost unconscious when he felt the ship accelerating.

Chapter Twenty-Seven

Logan slowly woke to the sound of alarms. Groggy and disoriented, it took him a minute to remember where he was. When it hit him he was on a space ship headed into deep space, he took a gasping breath. How long had he been out?

He was still wearing his space suit, but the face plate was up. He rotated his head to examine the room and saw Knock sitting in the captain's seat with his eyes closed. The foam encasing him was dissipating rapidly. When it was gone, he unbuckled the safety harness and slowly climbed out of the seat. His legs felt like rubber and he stumbled. Using the backs of the control seats as handholds, he made his way toward Knock. His friend's eyes fluttered open but Logan hardly noticed. A huge reddish brown planet filled the view port. Gliese 667 if the ship had taken them where he'd directed it.

"Dude, where we at?" Knock asked.

Logan pointed to the view screen.

"Is that what I think it is?"

"Not sure," Logan said. "I think the ship took off in hyper drive and we're staring at Gliese."

"I'm freaking starving," Knock said. "How long have we been out?"

"Not sure, but we better get all this straight pretty darn quick, because if that is Gliese, the Company will know we're here and we'll be miners before we know what hit us."

They looked at each other and said, "Eddie!" at the same time.

Knock struggled out of his seat and they wobbled out of the command center holding on to each other. The medical unit was down one floor. They took the stairs, a narrow circular set that took up very little space. By the time they were on the next floor, Logan's head had cleared. They really better hustle. The Company had great communications and would know all about who they were and what they'd done on the moon.

Logan led the way into the medical unit. The Re-Juve was just opening. The stretcher slid out of the Plexiglas tube and Eddie sat up good as new. "Where are we?"

"That's it?" Logan laughed. "Just where are we? Not how are you or what happened?"

"Obviously, I was in a state-of-the-art Re-Juve so we must be on a starship. Is it the Far Horizon?"

Logan nodded. "Yup and the planet in the view screen looks like pictures I've seen of Gliese 667. I tried to key the ship to go there, but I'm not as good as you with computers."

Eddie swung his legs off the stretcher. "Did any of the detainees make it?"

"Shayna and Raj took a bunch into the passenger hold to strap down," Knock said.

"Eddie, how long did the trip take? Do you know? It seems like only a few minutes."

"It took four hundred and eighty-three days," Eddie said. "Did the blast chairs surround you with blue stuff?"

Logan nodded.

"That's stas foam. It puts you into a state of suspended animation until the trip is over. These big Company ships are all computerized."

"Well they must know who we are and what we did," Knock said. "So, uh, we better think of something fast."

"We need to eat first and check on the passengers," Eddie said. "The Re-Juve was feeding me through a tube," he rubbed his throat, "But I'm still starving."

They raced out of the medical unit and into the main passageway. The ship was shaped a lot like a tube with four levels. This level contained the medical unit and crew quarters along with a cafeteria for feeding the crew. The passengers were all on the second level and the engines and cargo space on the bottom which was the first level. They found the cafeteria easily by the smell of food cooking. When the ship woke them up, it also began cooking meals for them.

Logan stood looking at the trays of waiting food sitting on a metal counter in front of slots. "This is just like the food servo units in apartments on Earth," Eddie said. "There's not much we can eat without being poisoned."

Logan examined each tray and grabbed a fully hydrated banana. He stuffed it into his mouth. "This is okay," he mumbled.

Eddie pushed through some swinging doors into the preparation area and found a freezer. Inside, cases of food were stacked on metal shelves. Frozen vegetables were stacked by themselves along with cases of fruit. "As long as this hasn't been cooked or repurposed, we can eat it," he said and tore into a case of frozen strawberries.

Logan read the side of one of the tubs. "Sweetened," he said, disgusted and dropped it.

They ended up with more bananas, some raw carrots and potatoes stored in a cooler along with heads of wilting cabbage. There were bags of apples there as well. They ate until they'd had enough. "We gotta bounce," Logan said. "We're all in trouble up here. Just sittin' ducks waiting for the hunters."

They descended to the next floor and found Shayna and the rest of the passengers just waking up. Shayna spotted Logan when he emerged from the lift and ran to him. She's shucked her spacesuit and wore a big smile. "Are we here? Are we on another planet?"

Raj elbowed past a knot of gawking passengers to grab Logan. "You did it, man. We're free."

"Not yet," Logan said as he wrapped one arm around Shayna and stared at the gathered passengers. "Folks, we are currently orbiting Gliese 667 . . . if I got it right." He glanced at Eddie. "So, how do we land?"

At that moment a loud clanging began. A huge holo screen overhead lit up with the face of a Company man wearing a mining officers' uniform. "Passengers aboard Far Horizon, this is the commander of Mining Camp 405, Colonel Randal Cummings, prepare to be boarded. You have entered Gliese-controlled space and are on an unapproved flight plan."

"Eddie," Logan said.

"Bridge!" Eddie shouted and took off for the lift.

"Take the passengers to the next level and get them some food," Logan said to Shayna. "We pulled some Sopore-free vegies and fruit out of the freezers and cooler, but be careful what you eat." He pointed to them. "It probably doesn't matter what they eat. They will go into withdrawal if they don't get some Sopore anyway."

She nodded and unable to help himself, he kissed her. She touched the side of his face gently and he read in her eyes what he'd been looking for all his life. "Be careful," she whispered.

He grinned his cockiest smile and she returned it. "Of course."

He took off after Eddie and Knock leaving Shayna to manage the passengers with Raj's help. Once inside the bridge, Logan saw a Company ship through the view screen closing in on the Far Horizon.

Eddie was in the captain's seat. His hands flew across the blinking control panel. "I've taken control of the ship," he told Logan. "Get into the co-pilot's seat and give me a hand."

"What can I do?" Logan said in a small voice as he slid into the empty chair.

"Knock, get on the communications and try to locate a signal coming off the planet at 39.0997° N, 94.5783° W."

"What?" Knock looked totally confused.

"Coordinates," Eddie snapped. "Just key them into the unit." Eddie's hands flew across the control panel and the huge ship began a slow turn.

Logan stared at the control panel and at Eddie. "You know something," he finally said.

"There's a Tong spaceport at those coordinates."

"But the Tong is allied with the Company."

"Not officially so maybe they won't know about us yet. We only just got here. I'm going to send them a distress signal for help landing. Once we're on the ground we'll have to wing it."

"I got 'em!" Knock yelled from the com station.

Eddie waved his hand across the control array one more time and ran to Knock's seat. He brought up a holo screen, typed SOS on a virtual keyboard and hit send. "Keep hitting send until they reply," he told Knock and ran back to the captain's seat. He slapped one hand on the controller and banked the large ship. The rust-colored planet drew closer and as they shot through striated thin clouds Eddie leveled the ship. Details began appearing on the planet below. The mining town was clear and stretching for miles around were mountains of debris from the operation.

"Stop or we will open fire!" Erupted from Knock's com station and on the screen in front of him the angry face of Colonel Randall Cummings glared at them.

"Can he see us?" Logan asked Eddie.

Eddie went to the com and hit a switch. "Not any more. Ignore him."

"But they're going to shoot at us." Knock said.

"He can't. We're loaded with potential mining conscripts. That's what he wants. He's just gonna follow us and try to snag all of us when we land. As far as he's concerned, this is in the bag and we're already working in his mines."

Logan shuddered. "What we gonna do?"

Eddie's grim face hovered over the controls as he concentrated. "Whatever it takes."

"Does this tank we're riding in have weapons?"

"Nope," Eddie snapped.

A long string of Chinese erupted over the com. Logan snapped to attention. "That's the Tong. They want us to identify ourselves and state our problem and why we need their aid."

"You speak Chinese?" Eddie asked.

"I read it better, but Cantonese, yeah."

Eddie smiled. "Then switch places with Knock.

Logan and Knock switched seats. "Now what?"

"Key the com and tell them we're coming in hot with a cargo of conscripts for the mines. Our steering system is broken can they send us a directional beam and land the ship."

"How can they do that?" Logan asked.

"Their computer talks to our computer, lands the ship," Eddie said.

"Do you think using the Tong for anything is a wise idea?" Knock asked.

Eddie turned and glared at him. "It's all we got unless you have a brilliant suggestion."

"I don't," Knock said. "But Helga might."

"Who?" Eddie asked.

Logan got out of the com seat and stared at Knock. "You brought her along, didn't you?"

Knock's face slowly turned the color of ripe apples. "Uh, maybe."

Eddie clambered out of the captain's chair and stared at Knock. "Who or what is a Helga?"

Knock took the cube out of his inside pocket and keyed it. The beautiful maid immediately appeared. "What would you like, master?"

Eddie's eyes popped open as wide as his Chinese ancestry would allow. "You have a holo maid?"

"It was Hump's," Knock muttered. "We have a relationship. I couldn't leave her behind, could I? Helga, can you land a space ship?"

"Of course, my good master." She walked to the control panel and passed her hands over them. "I am so sorry my master. We are already in a planet-side tractor beam which will guide the ship to a safe landing."

Eddie groaned. "Too late, but great idea, Knock."

"I can try to get them to release us," Logan said.

"Do it," Eddie told him.

Logan chattered away into the com unit in Cantonese. An immediate answer can back and Logan threw up his hands. "They know who we are."

Seconds later the ship made a shuddering turn and began descending. "They got us," Eddie said. "We better get prepared and hit the cargo deck."

"We are so screwed." Logan moaned.

Eddie's smile was grim. "We have to make the best of it, defend ourselves and make a run for it. Maybe they don't have the whole story and it will only be the locals because the Company hasn't had time get there. We should be able to handle a few men."

As they headed out of the bridge, Logan bumped Knock's arm. "Helga? Really, dude."

They ran down the stairs to the third floor. Shayna met them outside the cafeteria. "What's happening? I felt the ship turn."

"The Tong space port has us in a directional beam," Eddie said. "They'll land us, but we need to be ready to run the minute we land."

"Will they be armed?" Knock asked.

"Yeah," Eddie said. "But they won't be expecting us to be hostile unless they're in touch with the Colonel, which I doubt, because even though the Tong is working with the Company, it's a pretty closely-held secret and they aren't supposed to be working directly with the Company ever. Their association is strictly off the books."

"And if they do know?"

"Let's raid the ship's arsenal."

"They have one?"

Eddie grinned. "Of course."

"I'm going with you," Shayna said.

"Me, too," Raj said.

They found the arms locker outside the bridge. Eddie opened it by using Logan's level-five key and they each took a blaster, a stunner and extra ammo packs. Body armor hung from pegs. Logan handed everyone a vest. "This is serious. If we get fired on, let me and Knock handle it. You guys hang back. We'll be the soldiers. We need Eddie's knowledge and Shayna, you have to take care of the passengers. Raj, you're just too young."

"No I ain't." Raj puffed out his thin chest.

Knock shoved him toward the lift. "Yes you are, but come with us anyway."

The ship leveled and the Tong spaceport emerged from the clouds fully visible. It was small with one junker Tong ship sitting on the launch pad. There was one metal building and a host of tents. As they drew closer to the ground, Logan saw small people running toward an open piece of tarmac. "Looks like we're getting a welcoming committee."

Chapter Twenty-Eight

Dek glanced into the lavender sky and shaded his eyes from the glare of the sun. Overhead, a huge Company ship slowly descended toward the spaceport. He and his people were all packed and ready to head to a new location about fifty miles to the west. The spaceport was just too dangerous. They needed to put some distance between them.

"What in the hell is that?" Cain Hollyroad asked as he dragged a load of equipment to the wooden sled they had constructed. He stood next to Dek and stared into the sky.

"That, my friend, is a conscript carrier full of brand new slaves for the mine."

"Why they landing here?"

"Good question and one I think we should investigate."

Mai put her small hand in his. "Do you think there is some kind of problem with the ship?"

Dek squeezed her shoulder. "Could be, but I think we should check this out. It's the first time I've heard of a Company ship landing anywhere but the Company spaceport."

"If there's something wrong, the Company will send people here" she said with real panic in her voice.

"Don't worry. You and the family will be long gone and safe." He glanced at Cain. "I got a feeling this could be something interesting."

Cain groaned. "I hate when you get those feelings."

Dek lifted one large finger. "I know, but, this I think is something we can't let go by without checking into."

Cain grinned. His big smile cracked the tanned skin of his square-jawed face. "If it's Company business, maybe we can disrupt some of their plans."

Dek nodded. "Every chance we get as long as it doesn't endanger the family." He turned and glanced back at the rest of their people, Tom, Terrance, the women and two recent escapees who had found them a week ago. "Tell Tom to get everyone started for the new camp," he said to Mai Li. "We'll be along directly."

"You take care of yourself," she admonished. "Where would I be without you?"

He pecked her cheek and went to pick up his M-32p5. "Grab the blaster and let's go," he said to Cain.

"The blaster?"

"Yeah, the blaster. I got me a feeling about this."

They jogged up the mountain where they'd killed the loris only a few months ago. Dek was in the best shape he'd been in since the military. He might be fifty, but he could still do a one-handed pullup carrying his pack and run all day. At the top of the mountain he stopped and looked up. The huge Company ship seemed so close he could reach up and touch it. The ship flew over the mountain and began to settle on the open tarmac. There was only one Tong ship in the spaceport, but the usual complement of riffraff had flooded the tarmac from the tents and the one metal building.

Dek used the field glasses to scan the horizon for any other ships. Far in the distance, he saw the contrail of a big, fast ship headed this way. "Looks like something is really wrong," Dek said. "They got a Company battle cruiser after them."

"What you thinkin'?"

Dek laid the barrel of the M-32p5 across his left arm. "I'm thinkin' that ship down there is running from the Company and might need our help."

"Who might need our help?"

"The conscripts. That's a conscript carrier filled with people dragged from their lives on Earth. There have to be Vagrants and mole people on board. Who else could they be bringing here? And those, my friend, are our people."

Cain's mobile left eyebrow shot up. "How are we gonna take care of a whole load of conscripts? We can barely take care of ourselves."

Dek started down the other side of the mountain toward the spaceport. "If we don't help them, how can we claim to be humans? There's no question of whether we should, Cain, only how can we?"

Mumbling and grumbling Cain followed. "This is gonna be fun."

Dek smiled. "You know, I think it is."

Logan, Raj, Knock and Shayna stood at the cargo port waiting for the ship to settle. They were already on land, but the ship still felt like it was floating. As it slowly dropped the last foot Logan looked at Knock. "You ready for this?"

Knock's lopsided grin said everything. "It's been great knowing you, dude, and what an adventure we've had."

Shayna slapped his shoulder. "Don't talk like that."

As the structure of the ship groaned and settled, Logan took a deep breath and stared straight ahead. The cargo hold doors suddenly creaked and groaned and started opening. They heard the latches clang and a sliver of crazy lavender-blue sky peeped in at the top of the door. When the door hit the ground, he and Knock stepped forward onto the ramp. The people waiting outside were from the dregs of society. Surely none of them had chips or credit discs. For a moment, Logan felt hope blossom in his chest, and then he spotted Benny Ho and five Tong spacers closing in through the crowd.

"What do we do Logan?" Knock whispered.

"Stay calm. Let's try to bargain with him."

"Well if it ain't the little turd who stole Tong gold delivered right into my hands like a Christmas present. Long Sam still want his money, mole boy. You got it?"

"I gave you two bars of gold, Mr. Ho. Isn't that enough to buy my way out of here?"

The huge man laughed and his whole body shook like jelly. Overhead, the Company battle cruiser began its landing approach. Panic filled Logan. He glanced first at Ho and then the cruiser. They were in a terrible mess. He was in a terrible mess. If they didn't get gobbled up by the Tong, the Company would surely do it. He pointed his blaster at Benny Ho. "We're going to walk out of here right now, all of us, or I'm going to shoot you."

The five Tong spacers behind Ho all pulled blasters out of battle holsters and pointed them at Logan and Knock. "No you ain't," Ho snarled. He stomped up the ramp and snatched the blaster out of Logan's slack grip while one of his henchman snagged the one out of Knock's. Shayna and Raj handed theirs over without a whimper. They were done, toast, finished. The bitter taste of defeat stung Logan's mouth as his heart fell to his feet. They had fought their way to this point for nothing. His friends would surely go to the mines and he, well he was destined to live out the rest of his miserable life, and it wouldn't be a long one, as a Tong slave.

When he turned to say as much to Knock, a bullet slammed into Ho and knocked his gigantic body off the ramp. Shayna shrieked as two more Tong members were hit by the mysterious rounds of fire. Logan yelled for Knock to take cover back inside the ship. They scrambled for safety as more shots rang out and the riffraff following the Tong ran for their tents and the building. In seconds, the tarmac was clear.

Logan searched for the source of the fire and saw two men running toward them. Something about the way one of the men held himself and ran jogged a memory deep inside Logan. But it couldn't be. He turned to Knock. "Grab everyone and head for those two men!"

Knock took off, Logan grabbed Shayna's hand and shoved Raj after Knock. "Hurry. The Company ship just opened its port."

The passengers flowed out of the ship and raced into the rusty landscape heading toward the two men who had stopped and were providing cover fire. Logan jogged toward the two men as though in a dream. How could this be happening? How had it happened? One of the men stepped forward and the other began hustling the refugees up the side of the mountain. The man who stepped forward was Logan's father. He'd know that tall, broad-shouldered figure anywhere.

"Dad?" Logan's voice cracked.

"Logan? Is that really you?"

His father rushed forward and grabbed him in a bear hug. Tears rolled down Logan's face unchecked and unheeded. "Dad, Dad, how can you be here?"

His father held him at arm's length and stared at his face with tears in his eyes. "You've grown so much," he sobbed. "You look so much like your mother."

A rock exploded, shocking them out of the moment. Dek grabbed Logan's arm. "Run!"

Logan looked once over his shoulder and saw a group of Enforcers surging out of the battle cruiser. They still weren't safe, but he trusted his father.

They passed the last of the passengers and made it to the front. "Help them over the top, Cain. Logan and I will cover you guys."

Cain lifted an eyebrow but handed his blaster to Logan. They took up a position behind some rocks. When the last of the passengers including Shayna and Raj were over the top, the first of the Company Enforcers were within range. "Hold your fire, son," Dek said as he began picking the Company men off one at a time. After the first two fell to Dek's incredibly accurate sniper fire, the Enforcers stopped and raced back down the slope. There was no cover. They were easy pickings. Dek winged two more, knocking them down with his large caliber ammo. When the Enforcers were running for their lives in a full retreat, Dek grabbed Logan's hand. "Bought us some time, son, but they'll regroup and be back. We need to go."

They followed the group of passengers over the top of the mountain. Cain had them bunched up in what looked like the remains of some kind of camp or primitive village. He'd done a head count. "We got us fifty-two, Dek," he said. "What's your plan?"

Shayna left the group and put her arm through Logan's.

"And who might this be?" Dek said with a grin.

Logan threw his chest out and returned the smile. "This is Shayna Nagata. She's my girlfriend."

"You got great taste in women, boy. Now, do any of these folks have talents or skills we can use?"

Logan nodded. "They're Vagrants, Dad, survivors like you and me. Just tell us where to go and what to do. I promise we won't be a burden."

He raised his hand and the escaped Company prisoners all hushed. "This is my father, Deklan Hall. He's going to help us get away. You with us?"

The passengers cheered.

Dek pointed down a path heading toward the river. "Then let's get going."

Logan hugged Shayna. "We got us a new life and a new dream. You with me?"

She lifted her face and stared into his eyes. "Forever."

Gabe Thompson has a degree in journalism and currently teaches school in Jacksonville, Florida where he lives with his wife and twelve-year old son. While he lives in Florida, he's traveled the world. He draws upon his experiences in life as fodder and inspiration for writing. He retired from the military because of medical reasons, but regularly flies around the world on military Space A, AMC and MAC flights. The military has bases in some of the best places. Gabe plans on venturing to most of them before he dies. He has three blogs on Wordpress. You can connect with him there.

http://www.gabethompson.wordpress.com

http://ilovebookreviews.wordpress.com/

http://everythingya.wordpress.com/

Tell-tale Publishing would like to thank you for your purchase. If you would like to read more by this or other fine TT authors, please visit our online store:

www.tell-talepublishing.com

59415475R00142

Made in the USA
Lexington, KY
04 January 2017